ZUG ISLAND

A Detroit Riot Novel

GREGORY A. FOURNIER

Zug Island: A Detroit Riot Novel

Published by Wheatmark®
610 East Delano Street, Suite 104, Tucson, Arizona 85705 U.S.A.
www.wheatmark.com

Original cover design by Carole Lecren.
Cover photo by Bill Deneau.

ISBN: 978-1-60494-585-0 (paperback)
ISBN: 978-1-60494-608-6 (Kindle)
LCCN: 2011925408

Acknowledgments

M*y heartfelt thanks to* those who gave of their time and effort to offer insights and suggestions which helped me bring my novel to completion: Beverly Fitzsimons, Linda Joyce, and Victoria Campbell, my Detroit connection; David L. Poremba of the Detroit Public Library for his background materials on Zug Island; and a special thanks to Carleen Hemric and Lindsay Barrett, who have stuck with me from the beginning of this project and whose advice and motivation have been invaluable.

Contents

I dedicate this novel to the memory of the forty-three people who lost their lives in the Detroit riots and to the recovery of Detroit, a wounded city still struggling for its survival.

Introduction

D*ownriver from the city* of Detroit, just south of historic Fort Wayne, lies a stretch of marshland that was once the site of ancient Native American burial grounds now known as Zug Island. Samuel Zug, a successful Detroit furniture maker and founder of Michigan's Republican Party, bought the 325 acres in 1876 as a real estate investment to provide security for his wife, Ann.

He envisioned building a luxurious estate on the waterfront, but the couple abandoned their home after ten years because of the dampness which bred biting mosquitoes, croaking frogs, and persistent mildew. The property also contained a sulfur spring which bubbled up 1,200 barrels of mineral water per day and oozed its way into the swift-running Detroit River.

In 1888, Mr. Zug allowed the Rouge River Improvement Company to cut a canal known as Mud Run—sixty feet wide and five feet deep—through his land to connect the Rouge River with the Detroit River at the north end of the property, making it a man-made island. Three years later, he made the real estate deal of the decade by selling his island for 300,000 dollars, to be used as a dumping ground to fill in the marshland and bring the land above the water table, making it suitable for industrial use.

In 1901, seventy-five acres were sold to Detroit Southern Railroad, which established coal docks there. Four months later, New York capitalists invested $750,000 to build two blast furnaces on the island and create the Detroit Iron and Steel Plant. By 1926, Zug Island was supplying Detroit industry with molten pig iron to be processed into high-quality carbon and cold-rolled steel for the burgeoning automobile business. Zug Island's blast furnaces also produced and supplied structural steel, helping to fuel America's industrial revolution of the twentieth century. Detroit Iron and Steel was eventually sold to Great Lakes Steel, a division of the National Steel Corporation.

During World War II, Great Lakes Steel added a third blast furnace on Zug Island, the largest blast furnace in the world at the time with an annual output of 450,000 tons, almost 50 percent of the island's capacity to fuel the war effort. Their huge mills turned out high-tensile and alloy steel for tanks, airplanes, guns, ships, helmets, bombshell casings, and bullets for the nation's defense, helping earn Detroit the title of "The Arsenal of Democracy."

The once-thriving marshland and ancient burial grounds for many tribes of local Native Americans no longer supports the variety of plant and animal life that nature had preordained. The home of black bear, whitetail deer, mallard ducks, blue herons, mud hens, and muskrats is lost forever, forfeited in the name of human progress.

Samuel Zug died in 1896, at the age of eighty, leaving a dump as his memorial. He never lived to see the mighty industrial complex that to this day bears his name. And of the roughly two thousand people who work there at any given time, nobody gives a good goddamn either.

1 The Village Idiot

By *1967, growing up* young and stupid in the Detroit area was a time-honored tradition, but I felt like I was dumber than most eighteen-year-old rutting males. After an ill-fated first semester at Eastern Michigan University, I was unceremoniously exiled from the ivy-covered walls of academia at the behest of the dean of liberal arts himself, Dean Arthur Waterston.

I think the dean was trying to help me and Russell, my partner in crime. We were accused of drinking on campus, and he seemed troubled at the prospect of suspending us from college.

Sitting across from us, behind his executive desk, Dean Waterston asked, "Before I make my final decision about this unfortunate situation, I need to know whether there are any mitigating circumstances." From his brief inquiry into the matter, he knew that other students were allegedly involved, and we were likely innocent bystanders taking the fall for them. But he wanted to know why.

Russ and I sat there speechless and embarrassed. Yes, others had been involved; in fact, they were guilty of this particular charge. Yet Russ and I had been drinking beer and mixed drinks at a friend's apartment party that December Saturday night, to blow off some steam before semester exams in another week or so. When the booze ran out and the party died down, we returned to our dorm room to sleep it off.

Our dormitory suite mates, who had partied in their adjoining room while we were off campus, had created a disturbance and a noise complaint at 10:45. The dorm manager brought the campus police down on us sometime after 11:15. The police found some empties in the room adjoined to ours, and these other idiots had the good fortune to be on another beer run when the campus cops arrived and entered their room through their unlocked door. They got off scot-free. Coming through the bathroom into our dark room, the cops lit up our faces with their flashlights. Naturally, we smelled like a brewery, and the bright light further disorientated us as we both had fallen soundly asleep. Our guilt seemed clear. Case closed. That's how it looked in the report anyway.

Dean Waterston picked up a letter from the folder on his tidy desk and read it silently for a minute.

Looking up slowly he said, "Your dorm manager says you are the two nicest guys in your dorm and that you may be covering up for others. What about it?" He slid his bifocals down the bridge of his nose and peered over the rims of his glasses. "Is there any truth to this?" Waterston had a calm, direct style that I admired. Really, I couldn't make myself dislike the man. He knew we weren't coming clean with him, and he wanted us to spill our guts, but we weren't cooperating.

Growing up in the Detroit area, I guess Russ and I had seen one too many Warner Bros. gangster movies on the *Bill Kennedy Afternoon Movie* television show because we decided to uphold the most sacred commandment of the street, "Don't be a squealer!" The Dead End Kids would have been proud. We sat there like a couple of village idiots and lightly shrugged our shoulders while the others went on with their college plans.

"Apparently, your dorm manager, Mr. Le Claire," the dean said referencing the letter, "has discovered some information contrary to the initial police report. But he doesn't name names. It is up to you two to fill in the blanks, so we can get to the bottom of this incident and move on." The dean casually tossed the report on his desk. "So, what do you say?"

Waterston pushed his high-backed leather chair away from his desk, unbuttoned his suit coat, and did everything but roll up his sleeves to make us feel comfortable. This guy was great! He looked across the desk at us. Russ was gazing down, fixated on his shoes, but when the dean looked directly at me I simply raised my eyebrows and lightly shrugged my shoulders again. I reasoned that whether we rolled over on the others or not, we were still in trouble. "I've got nothing to add."

That was not the answer the dean wanted to hear, but he washed his hands of the matter. "All right then. In light of everything I know about this incident," he said, "I'm placing you both on social probation for a semester. If you want to come back, you'll need to reapply for the fall semester." He held out his hand for us to shake and left us with this small comfort: "Don't be discouraged, boys. This episode is merely a bump in the road of life. I sincerely hope you both will continue your education."

We both thanked him and quietly closed the heavy oak door on our way out of his office. With that, we were kicked out of college and thrust into the "real world," a place we had heard about from our teachers, whose job it was to keep it at arm's length from us. Russ joined the air force, and I got fitted for a blue collar.

My steamer trunk, so carefully packed by my proud mother only months before, stood unexpected and silent on the landing next to my neighborhood

Ecorse, several miles up the road, where the business offices and main steel-fabrication plants were located.

Steelworkers didn't make as much money as auto workers, but the pay was the best I could hope for, being an unskilled and inexperienced high school graduate in the dead of winter. I drove from the employment office to the main plant and was given a clutch of paperwork and directions to someplace called Zug Island. Turns out that working there was the best education I ever had.

Soon I found myself driving through the soot-encrusted neighborhood of Delray in southeast Detroit. Delray once hosted a thriving Hungarian community anchored by an impressive Catholic church, St. John's, now battered and boarded up. The neighborhood, long abandoned for the suburbs, was eventually strangled off by the triple threat of urban blight, white flight, and heavy industry. Other than a few tenement flop houses and a handful of struggling businesses, the tavern was the only establishment making any money. The bar served mainly steelworkers, who were always thirsty.

I continued driving up West Jefferson Avenue until I came to a large sign that had "Zug Island" painted on it and a large black arrow pointing right. I made a hard turn, weaving and sliding my way down the icy pot-hole-damaged road bordered by security fences and the Solvay Chemical Works plant. The road bent to the right and led to a trestle bridge that crossed over to the island beyond which a towering blast furnace loomed. I braked for the biggest red light I had ever seen.

Some island! Barely a moat, more like a drainage ditch, separated Zug Island from the slum of Delray. The bridge was barely a semi's width, with a railroad track running down its center. It was so narrow that traffic could go only one way at a time. Drivers could either leave the island or wait to come onto the island. Giant-sized traffic signals controlled the flow of vehicles from each end of the bridge, but trains always had the right-of-way, so drivers had to pay attention. I waited until several semis crossed over the bridge; on the green signal I drove onto the island. I turned right and parked near the front entrance. I was directed by a security guard in a small booth to the personnel and first-aid offices. He sized me up quickly and pointed me in the right direction before I could ask for directions.

In the personnel office, I gave my job referral from the state employment office to a clerk, and she gave me more paperwork to fill out. I needed to take my prehire physical and complete some employment paperwork—my United Steelworkers union membership application and monthly dues payment authorization; my benefits package signatures: health insurance, dental, accidental death, and next-of-kin notifications; and my federal withholding tax forms, my state of Michigan tax forms, and my Social Security tax forms.

Even with all of that, I was happy to be working and hoped that after everything was deducted from my first check, I'd have something left over to show for two weeks' work.

Half a dozen other white guys were filling out the same forms. This took about twenty minutes, and then we were called into an examination room. After a routine physical, we had our photos taken and identification badges made; then we were given our work gear, assignments, and reporting times. Great Lakes Steel was a huge and spread-out plant, and I was buried in the northern reaches of it. Where the other new hires went, I couldn't say. I never saw any of them again.

By the time I returned home later that afternoon, I was relieved and excited that I had finally found a job. I proudly showed my mother my identification badge and my work gear: a pair of Red Wing steel-toed boots, a red hardhat with a green cotton liner and a heat shield, wraparound safety glasses, heavy-duty leather work gloves, and an asbestos fire-resistant jacket.

"Well, what do you think?" I asked as I tried everything on for the first time.

"Son, you be careful and watch yourself over there."

"Mom, don't worry! That's why they gave me all this safety gear," I said, lacing up my boots and standing before her. I felt like a fully suited hockey player.

"Zug Island is a dangerous place. It's the filthiest hellhole in the city."

"Yeah, what do you know about it?" I was surprised she even knew the name of the place.

Looking at me fully ensconced in my work attire, she said with a staid expression, "I remember your father in the same getup twenty years ago."

On my first workday at Zug Island, I stepped out of my car into the early morning darkness. The arctic express came barreling down from the Canadian north, rifling through the strait separating Detroit from Windsor. When I started walking, I was conscious of two things: the sound of crunching snow dusted over with grey soot and the stench of steelmaking that hung in the predawn air like a foul vapor. I began work a week after New Year's Day. I didn't know exactly where I was going, so I gave myself some extra time to puzzle it out and arrived at quarter past five in the morning, although the day shift started at six. In the darkness, the island looked mysterious and foreboding. As I had done on the first day, I asked the security guard in his booth for directions.

"Hey, I'm just starting work today and—" I yelled above the wailing and moaning wind.

Without opening the door, I barely heard the

security guard say, "No shit!" He looked annoyed at me standing there all spick-and-span. I had disturbed him as he huddled over a small electric heater in his booth. "Go to battery two!" he barked. When I looked bewildered, he grimaced and pointed impatiently. "Follow the goddamned road," he snapped.

I pointed down the road.

He bobbed his head up and down several times. "Yes! Yes, you moron!"

I followed some tire grooves cut into the snow and ice. The mercury couldn't have been more than ten degrees above zero that morning, with a wind chill wavering between ten and fifteen below. The wisps of blowing snow felt more like they were sandblasting my face than dainty crystalline structures wafting through space. The wind cut through my Levis and thermal long underwear as if I were wearing lightweight linen trousers. Steam rose from a huge pile of smoldering coke along the roadside disappearing into the morning air robbed of its warmth.

Zug Island is a relic of a faltering smokestack technology we now call the rust belt. Just four miles south of downtown Detroit in the city of River Rouge, the alchemy of steel making takes place. Two coke plants convert train car loads of ground coal into tons of hotter and cleaner burning chunks of coke to feed the island's three hungry blast furnaces twenty-four hours a day, three hundred and sixty-five days a year. It is a nonstop operation. Huge vertical ovens set side by side bake the impurities out of the coal, and the coke gets pushed out of each oven into a hot car after baking for twenty to thirty hours. Progress never sleeps.

I began to follow some railroad tracks which materialized in the foreground but disappeared into the murky shadows of the towering blast furnaces in the distance to the left. Suddenly, black-and-white striped railroad gates lowered into position. The flashing red lights and clanging signal bells startled me, and I lurched backwards and felt my feet slip out from under me. I fell ass-over-heels on the roadway, denting my new aluminum lunchbox. Feeling foolish, I picked myself up, brushed off the snow and ice, and stood marching in place to warm myself while waiting for the train cars to pass.

Where are the other guys I hired in with? I thought. The place looked deserted like some post-apocalyptic ruin. My toes were already numb from intense cold and lack of circulation. *What am I doing here? Damn it! Now, I have to pee.* No one was around, so I walked behind some stacked barrels to get out of the wind, took off my gloves, and worked my way through the layers of my clothing. Close call—I barely got my unit out before wetting myself. I watched precious warmth rise from the stream, leaving me even colder than before, not to mention exposing another part of my body to frostbite.

What the hell am I doing here? I repeated to myself.

Zug Island was a far cry from the toasty lecture halls I had haunted just a short month before, but now college life seemed distant and dreamlike, an alternate reality of promise and deferred gratification wrapped in a warm goose-down featherbed.

The railroad tracks announced the approach of an odd-looking train, accompanied by the rhythm of its steel wheels creaking and squeaking along the frozen tracks. Bottle cars lumbered past, each brimming with molten pig iron heading for the steel-refining plant in Ecorse, four miles down the rail line. I waited while a long string of these train cars passed by.

Standing there, I let my mind wander to distract me from the cold. I felt like I was caught between the pages of Dante's *The Inferno*. The Bible doesn't say much about hell, but Dante was haunted by it. A sign above the Gate of Hell read something like, "All ye who enter here, abandon hope." This warning seemed to apply to me in my present circumstance. I needed my own Virgil to lead me through this frozen wasteland to the coke ovens somewhere beyond.

It struck me how classic literature can speak across the ages in uniquely personal ways. The literary concept of universality was finally real to me. Suddenly, I wanted to be back at college in the worst way, living the good life, but then I was drawn by the same dread that Dante must have felt.

What am I doing here? How badly do I need the money? What are my other options? My answers were rehearsed and ready: *Make some quick money. Buy a nice car. Return to college.*

Despite the freezing temperature, my toes were sweating in my wool socks. I hadn't even started working yet and I felt miserable. If I hadn't backed myself into a corner over this school bullshit, I would have turned around and gone back to my warm bed after eating a steaming bowl of oatmeal. *But jobs are scarce in Detroit this time of year.*

Besides, my mother had made it quite clear that being a lounge lizard was not an option. She was still upset—not just about the waste of money or the government grant that I'd lost; she had bragged that I was the first person in the family to go to college, and now I had blown it.

"What am I going to tell the family?" she had said, shaking her head.

"Tell them I decided to be a factory rat like everyone else," I responded which angered her further. *Yep! I needed this job badly.*

The train finally crossed the roadway and curved into the darkness as I continued following the frozen truck ruts. After several more minutes, I saw two large and long rectangular buildings ahead in the distance. Naturally, the furthest away was Battery Two where I had been assigned. I wiggled my toes to make sure they still functioned and walked in that direction. The south end of Zug Island had several more strands of crisscrossing rail tracks that looked like heavy steel yarn tangled by some restless giant. Again, I thought of *The Inferno*.

I continued walking down the frozen road until I saw the coke ovens clearly as the sky slowly lightened. Each coke battery had eighty or more ovens lined up end to end, each about two feet wide and about twenty feet tall. A length of rail track ran parallel to the ovens for a hot car to run up and down to catch the tons of white orange, hot coke each oven held. Then the hot car would run into a water tower at the west end of the battery, called a quenching station, to drench its glowing load. A colossal white steam cloud hissed and rose from the hollow tower and rained frozen droplets over the surrounding area. In warm weather, the environment could adequately handle these repetitive showers; in subfreezing weather, the water froze in layers making it hazardous and damned near impossible to walk.

Icicles surrounded what looked like the only way up onto the platform where I could hear the ovens roar. A flash-frozen steel ladder appeared to be the last obstacle before I could report to my workstation. Cautiously, I kicked away some ice with my steel-toed boots, got my footing, and inched my way up, rung by rung, holding on for dear life. With my lunch box in hand, I carefully climbed to the concrete walkway above.

The shimmering waves of radiating heat from the coke ovens embraced the nearby air and gave me some welcomed relief from Jack Frost's biting lash. I walked alongside the ovens, warming myself, until I discovered a dimly lit bare lightbulb over the supervisor's office door at the midpoint of the divided battery. With my free gloved hand, I reached for the doorknob. There was no turning back now.

2

A Hazy Shade of Welcome

I *entered the office amidst* swirling snow and a frosty back wind. When I opened the door, a gust caught it and tore the knob from the stiff grip of my leather gloves and the oversized door blew wide open. A grey-haired, elderly man in a white helmet stood hunched over his desk with his arms spread out, securing a stack of blueprints so they wouldn't be blown about. Another man, a middle-aged black man in a yellow helmet, was leaning up against a row of file cabinets across the room. He was the first to greet me.

"Son of a bitch! Shut that goddamned door!" I soon found out he was the shift foreman and my immediate boss. He looked half asleep, but the cold blast had perked him up.

"I'm sorry," I said pulling the door shut with some difficulty.

"My, oh my … Reinforcements?" he said showing me some interest.

The old man raised his eyes from the blueprints and regarded me silently through soiled bifocals. I had the strange feeling he could read me easier than he could read the smudged blueprints on his desk.

I pulled the glove from my shivering right hand, reached inside my jacket, and offered the supervisor my paperwork. "I was told to report here this morning." The old man took the slip, looked at me again, and grinned. "Am I in the right place?" I asked. He sat down and rotated in his chair and hung his arm behind the backrest of his seat. He crossed his legs and examined me carefully, saying nothing, just grinning. I felt uncomfortable, so I asked again, "Is this where I'm supposed to be?"

"Son," the foreman said from across the room, "looks like you're a long damned way from where you're supposed to be."

The old man sat quietly and smirked.

"You're all spit-and-polished and ready to go. Ain't you?" the foreman said jerking my chain for some reason. I had no choice but to play along. I must admit that I was the cleanest-looking person in the room. In fact, I was brand-spanking-new.

"Sure, I'm ready to start working. Tell me where I need to go and what I need to do."

"You're not allergic to grit and grime, are you?"

"Not that I'm aware of."

This act was getting old, even for the supervisor. "Son," he said, "you're a sight for sore eyes. We're shorthanded as usual this time of year."

The old man turned to answer the ringing phone. "Yeah ... I'm not sure ... What? You're shitting me .... All right, I'll look into it and get back to you soon .... Right!" He hung up and turned around in his chair.

"Sarge, we need a dig-out crew on Battery One. The wall between ovens 36 and 37 needs some fire-brick work done. Scare up a crew for some overtime from the next two shifts."

"Will do, boss."

"I'll work some overtime," I interjected.

Both men looked at me surprised. "You're pretty anxious, ain't ya?" The foreman was less interested in the supervisor's request for an overtime crew than he was in me. Something wasn't adding up for him. "Let's cut the shit. What's a white boy from the suburbs doin' at the mill, son?"

"Working, making money. What else?"

"I guess. You haven't even worked your first shift, and you want overtime. That's pretty spunky for a guy who can't hold onto a doorknob in a fair wind," he jested.

"Hey, I apologized for that already."

"Must be something else!" His left eye grew and his right eye narrowed like Popeye's, and I was tempted to laugh at him.

"I'm trying to kill some time and make some money. No mystery. That's it!"

"Oh, no! In the spring or the fall, you middle-class kids work for a month or two for some quick cash. But to start work here in the dead of winter, it hasta be somethin' else." He smelled that something wasn't right about me. "It's pure misery working these batteries in January and February. It can freeze the balls off a brass monkey, son. The only worse time is July and August when the heat will melt the dingleberries right off your ass."

"No shit!" My mild attempt at motif humor was lost on the foreman. The supervisor smiled though.

"You think I'm playin' with you, son? I need to know if you're goin' to quit on me in a week or if I should train you for a more regular job. Most white boys from the suburbs don't like to get dirt under their fingernails. They're afraid this coal dust won't wash off. Ya dig!"

The black foreman had reduced me to a cultural stereotype, and the irony stung and insulted me. "What my personal story is has nothing to do with whether I can work a shovel or not," I answered back. "And yes, I can dig!"

"I'm jus' wonderin' if you know what you're gettin' yourself in for."

"Yes. I've already been told."

"Oh, yeah? From who?"

His tone annoyed me, so I corrected his grammar. "From whom."

"You making fun of the way I talk?"

Verbal jousting with the foreman was a decidedly stupid thing to do, but I couldn't help it. We were enjoined. "Speak," I said.

"What?"

"'Speak.' I'm not making fun of the way you 'speak.' It's an automatic reflex. I'm an English major." *That will shut him up,* I thought. *Wrong!*

"Ooooh! A college boy. If you're so fuckin' smart, why ain't you there instead of here? And don't think to correct my speech again, son," he warned cocking his head to one side and wrinkling his forehead.

It was none of his damn business why I was there. And where did he get off calling me "son" all the time? I was about to say "Screw this job!" when the old man leaning low on the armrest of his chair broke in again.

"You're Hank's son. Aren't you?"

The foreman stopped giving me the third degree and arched his eyebrows which wrinkled his forehead. He was as surprised by this turn in the conversation as I was. "Yes. I guess I am."

"You're not sure?" He smiled. "And your grandfather was Pete."

"You knew him too?"

"No, he's a mind reader, son," the foreman countered.

The supervisor rose from his chair and reached his hand out for me to shake. When I saw his bowed legs and full smile, it struck me who he was. "You're Scotty. Right?"

"That's right!"

One of my earliest memories of Scotty was him on first base and my father on third working the double play when I was eight years old. It was under the lights and the mosquitoes ate me alive that night. A couple of years after that, Scotty and my dad competed against each other in a local bowling league championship game. It came down to the last frame. My father stood silent, waiting for the onlookers to hush. When he was ready, he began his approach and moved forward one step, his muscled left arm aiming the shot, pumping the ball forward slightly; on the second step, his arm brought the ball backwards and loaded it up with energy, held weightless for a split second at the top of its arc; approaching the foul line and whipping his arm forward on his third step, he threw the ball like a rolling freight train and scattered the echoing bowling pins with a vengeance, hooking his final strike to win the tournament. I remember the cheers and Scotty shaking hands with my dad to congratulate him like it was yesterday. I had proudly held the trophy on my lap as we drove home afterwards in my dad's new two-tone Edsel. *Good times*. It had been years since I had seen or even heard about Scotty. I felt more relaxed now.

"This boy's father worked here almost twenty years ago, Sarge. I met his grandfather here almost twenty years before that. Some of his uncles and cousins put in their time here too."

"Do tell."

"This young man comes from a long line of Zug Islanders, heaven help them. Don't worry, Sarge. Jake won't be afraid of the work or the dirt."

"Then the mill is in your blood, you might say," Sarge remarked extending his hand to me. It was the first time I ever had any physical contact with a black person.

Black people were rarely if ever seen in my neighborhood, unless it was one of the Motown groups on the *Boppin' with the Robin Show* on CKLW, a Canadian television station we could pick up on our side of the river.

"You might say that," I agreed. Sarge's handshake was firm and calloused.

"Welcome to Hell's Bakery, son."

"Thanks, sir."

"What's this 'sir' shit? Call me Sarge," he said. "Everybody does."

Scotty began to reminisce out loud. "Jake, your grandfather was some kind of fisherman. Walleye, muskie, trout, bass, jumbo perch, he could catch fish out of an empty bucket. We'd go up to Canada once a year and have a great time fishing or duck hunting together."

It was great to hear him talk about my grandfather, a man I barely knew. He had died when I was six, so my memories were as faded as the grainy and yellowed photographs I had seen of him and his buddies holding up stringers of fish. Those were the only pictures we had of my grandfather. I couldn't wait to get home to see if a young Scotty was in any of them. It struck me as strange that my dad never once spoke about his father—for good or bad. I wondered why.

Now, it was Scotty's turn to question me. "Your granddad was lucky enough to retire from this place. I remember that he didn't want his sons to work here, but they did. Your dad hated working here and couldn't wait to get the hell out. You're the last person I expected to walk through that door. Now—what are you doing here?"

I still didn't want to go into my personal circumstances with either of them, but this time the reply came easier with Scotty, though it was still my private business. "The military doesn't want me—flat feet—so I decided to make some decent money for my trouble. If I work enough double shifts and holidays, I can get myself a car by the end of summer. I'm driving my uncle's broken-down 1963 Rambler." They both sat quietly. My answer rang so hollow that I could hear the wind howling outside. "And I may return to college in the fall if I feel like it."

"That's it, by Jesus!" Sarge said slapping his thigh. "You got kicked out of college. Hell! What else could it be?"

"Not quite!" I offered. "I was placed on social probation."

"What the hell is that? You bang the college president's daughter?"

"No, my roommate, Russell, did that," I said. Actually, it was the provost's niece, but sometimes it's easier to leave off a detail or two when the truth is irrelevant anyway.

"You college boys think you got all the answers, don't ya?"

I threw the foreman a bone, "I was sort of ... drinking, but not on campus."

"Drinking and on probation! I'll be goddamned." He burst out laughing. "You'll fit right in here, son."

"Jake, Sarge will show you where to get started and introduce you to some of the crew."

"What will I be doing?"

"Digging out belts. Glamour work, son."

"Sarge, get this man a new shovel."

"A new shovel?" Sarge questioned. "Are you sure?"

"Fresh out of the box."

"If you say so, boss."

"By the way," Scotty replied. "Say hello to your

father for me. I haven't seen him since your family moved to Dearborn some years ago."

That had been seven years before.

"He passed away just over two years ago," I said.

Scotty's demeanor changed. "He must have been only in his forties."

"Yeah, forty-four."

"What did he die from?"

"Heart and lung disease, the family curse." Scotty didn't ask for any details, but I offered them anyway. "He was working the graveyard shift at a tool and die shop just before the Thanksgiving holiday. Driving down Michigan Avenue, he had a massive heart attack. Apparently, he managed to pull safely off the street into a parking lot. A policeman found him the next morning collapsed over the steering wheel with the car's engine still idling and the headlights dimming."

Scotty became sullen at the news. "I'm very sorry to hear that," he said. "Give my condolences to your mother."

"Thanks, I will."

"One more thing."

"Yeah, what?"

"Make your goddamned money and get the hell out of here as fast as you can, son."

Suddenly that word, *son,* struck a resonating chord with me.

3 Ascent into the Maelstrom

Sarge had been decorated with a Purple Heart during the Korean War for taking a round in the rear while training raw recruits in the field under fire. Those who survived, he turned into soldiers. Once, I asked him about Korea, and all he said was he had an Asian tattoo on his ass; then he showed me his scar. I can tell you, it wasn't pretty. One of the other workers told me he was decorated with a Silver Star in World War II, but he never talked about it. Being a foreman suited Sarge; the job fit him like a glove: some authority without ultimate responsibility. Most people liked and looked up to him. The loyalty he felt for his men, they felt for him.

He reached into a back corner behind the file cabinets and pulled a new shovel out of a box. I assumed that all new hires received a fresh shovel as part of their initial work gear, but being set aside in the supervisor's office should have indicated its importance—for laborers anyway. I put on my work gloves, slung the industrial-strength shovel over my shoulder, and followed Sarge into the brittle morning sunshine.

Clear, sunny days in the north are bitter cold in January, but this day had to be one for the record books. My nostrils stuck together when I breathed in, and my spit froze before it hit the ground. The shift had already begun, and most of the crew were working by now. I was on a guided tour, so I paid attention.

Sarge and I climbed an iron ladder to the top of the coke battery, where a huge coal hopper dropped ground coal on a synchronized timetable into each oven through three aligned holes on top of the battery; then the hopper backed off for the lidman to do his job. Each filler hole was about twelve inches in diameter and belched billowy brown, tar-heavy smoke from each open filler hole with a vengeance. The smoke looked as toxic as it smelled and helped explain why smog was such a problem in the city.

A lidman, in protective clothing worthier than mine, stood on wooden clogs that kept the heat from roasting his feet through his boots. His job was to drag a heavy steel cap that looked like a mini-manhole cover over each of the holes using a long iron bar hooked on one end with a handle bent into the other end of it. He caught a tab molded on the top of the cap with the hook and pulled it over the hole. Next, he shoveled some ground coal around the edges of the hissing cap to seal it and minimize the air pollution. Then he moved over to the next one and the next one all day long in succession. He had to work fast because of the heat, but he had ten or fifteen minutes between each oven to wait in relative comfort. The company provided salt pill dispensers, fresh lemons, and plenty of water to help fight dehydration.

Sarge pointed out a by-products plant across from the coke plant. Hissing and steaming pipes took exhaust gases and coal tar drawn from the ovens to the by-products plant where it was converted into other products—like dandruff shampoo, of all things. So the smell of industrial-strength Tegrin hung everywhere.

We quickly walked across the top of the ovens to the other side and looked over the railing. "See those sloping firebricks down there and that long roofed area behind it?" Sarge said pointing downward.

I nodded, "Uh-huh. Is that where I'm going to work?"

"No, that's semiskilled labor. You're in the labor pool."

"What's the difference?"

"You don't need to know the difference. Just listen for a minute! You'll be working that shovel soon enough."

I forgot the shovel on my shoulder. "Okay."

"That's called the wharf. That guy down there pulling those gates is the wharfman. He controls the flow of coke onto a rubber conveyor belt that stretches hundreds of feet up that covered ramp way. Then it's sorted for size and rerouted onto other conveyor belts and sent throughout the plant, wherever it's needed. Some of it goes directly into the blast furnaces yonder, some is loaded into open train cars, and some is stockpiled along the island's rear-access road.

"There's a back entrance?" I asked as if I had discovered some guarded secret. "I didn't know there was another way onto the island."

But Sarge kept pulling rank on me. "You've only been here an hour, hotdog. There's a whole lot you don't know. Listen up and maybe you'll learn something, whiz kid."

If he would answer some of my questions, I might also learn something, I thought.

"Along this wall of ovens is an oven door remover machine," he continued. "Look down there and watch for a couple of minutes."

The door machine ran on electric power and lumbered methodically on its own set of tracks which ran parallel to the coke ovens. A huge man sat at the controls of the door machine with its simple system of hydraulic levers inside the cab of this cumbersome vehicle. He aligned the door machine with a prescheduled oven and pulled a worn lever releasing two powerful clamps, one towards the top of the door and one towards the bottom. The clamps unlatched the door and pulled it away from the blazing oven. Then he repositioned the machine and lined up a huge hopper in front of the open oven to guide the blazing coke into the waiting hot car.

On the opposite end of the oven, removing the door was the same procedure, but this side had a monstrous ramming machine which pushed the glowing coke through the oven, out the hopper, and into the waiting hot car. Then the coke was rushed into the quenching station at the end of the battery for a quick douse with water; finally, the hot car backed up to the wharf to drop its steaming load. This process was repeated day and night to produce the coke that kept the rest of the plant operating; it was really dramatic and impressive, a regular Rube Goldberg machine. "Fascinating, when you think about it." I said.

"What?"

"Steelmaking."

"We don't make steel here, we make pig iron."

I was confused—I'd thought this was a steel mill—my expression must have shown it.

"Any questions?"

"I don't want to bother you."

"Shoot!"

"What's the difference between pig iron and steel?"

I thought Sarge might come unwired at that question, but he seemed glad that he knew something I didn't. He leaned in toward my ear, so he didn't have to compete as much with the wind. "Let's walk over to the east end of the battery, and I'll break it down for you."

I wondered if all new hires got such a detailed tour. I doubted it. We found a place more protected from the weather where it was easier to talk and the oven's warmth collected before it was whisked away on the wind. "See those huge rusty piles on the ore docks?"

I nodded.

"Those are mountains of iron pellets, each pellet about the size of a marble. Before the river freezes in the winter, we stockpile it. Basically, we mix coke, iron pellets, and limestone in a blast furnace and superheat them using natural gas which ignites the coke and melts the iron. The limestone liquefies and reacts with the impurities which float to the top of the molten mixture. You know that sickly smell that hits you when you first come onto the island?"

"The one that would gag a maggot? Yeah, now that you mention it. I didn't want to complain."

"That's from the slag. It's drained off the pig iron into large slag pits. While one pit is filling up, the other pit cools and hardens in the open air. After the furnace is tapped and the pig iron is poured into bottle cars, it's taken to the main plant to be refined into steel in an open-hearth furnace."

"What happens to the slag?"

"The hardened slag is ground up and used for playground gravel, highway construction, and landfills among other things."

"Interesting."

"Follow me."

Walking a step or two behind him, I wondered where Sarge was leading me. We went to the center of the coke battery until we reached another iron ladder. This was to be my first lesson. "Never step down a fixed ladder—it takes too much time and energy," Sarge said. "Gimme your shovel and pay attention!"

"Sure, here it is." I waited to be taught by the master.

"You take the shovel, then wedge your shoulder and chin on the handle near the neck where the face is connected. Got it?"

"My neck or the neck of the shovel?"

"The neck of the goddamned shovel! Like this!" He secured the shovel with his chin and shoulder, grabbed the handrails with each hand, and hopped on the same handrails with his feet to glide briskly down twenty feet of ladder. "You try it now!" he shouted, competing to be heard over the wind and the roar of the ovens. "Here!" he said, throwing the shovel up to where he had just come down.

"Me?" I pointed at myself. My fingers were stiff, not only from the cold but also from fear. As a kid, I had fallen out of a tree and dislocated my shoulder. I disliked heights and became a little woozy at the thought.

"Jesus Christ, son! What's the problem?" Sarge shouted up.

I held up my lunch box for him to see. *What was I supposed to do with it?*

Sarge motioned for me to toss it to him. I mustered what little courage I could and grasped both handrails. I set my boots on the rails as Sarge had done, closed my eyes, and sailed down. I realized when I hit bottom that he hadn't told me how to brake with my hands and feet. My boots struck the uneven surface of the ice, twisting my left ankle. "SHIT!" I shouted. I hadn't even started working, and I was already injured and in pain. *Nice going, asshole.*

"Not bad, for your first try. Now, take the shovel up there this time and try it again while I light my cigarette." Sarge hunched against the wall and struggled against the wind with his Zippo while I struggled up the ladder with the shovel wedged between my chin and shoulder grasping each handrail for dear life.

Climbing up the icy steel rungs with a tender ankle pissed me off. Each time I put weight on it, my ankle sang out in pain. *Is Sarge just playing with me, or is he teaching me something useful?* I couldn't decide, but I didn't want to trash my other ankle on this attempt.

At the top, I looked down and saw a wisp of bluish smoke. I snapped my helmet liner under my chin to keep my hardhat from falling off. With shovel secured and almost ready, I leapt. My body raced downward, but the end of the shovel handle hit one of the ladder rungs on the way down and tumbled straight for Sarge's head. I arrived a split second before it hit him. He lost his balance on the ice and fell face first on the frozen ground with his crushed cigarette still in his mouth. I fought to hold back my laughter and almost wet my drawers.

"Jesus fucking Christ!" he cursed, picking himself up. We made eye contact and both broke out laughing. It could have been worse. He could have been seriously hurt; I could have been fired on the spot; or he could have belted me with the broad end of the shovel. My ankle was still twisted, but it didn't hurt as much now, and my spirits were lifted. I picked up my lunch box. *Lead on, Macduff,* I thought.

"Let's walk over to the canteen. We can warm up in there and get some coffee." These were the most welcome words I had heard all morning.

Now I was walking together with him rather than following behind. It felt better that way.

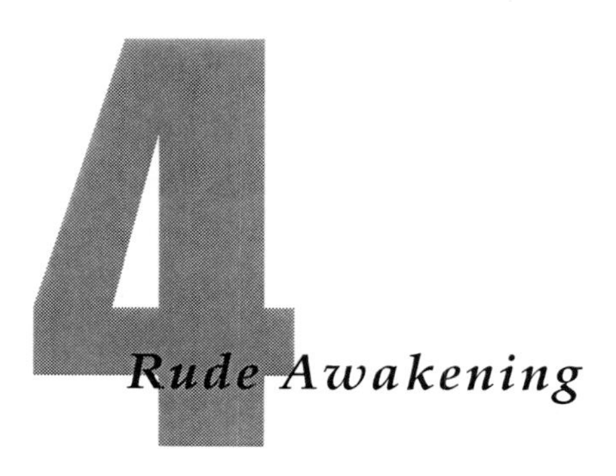

4 Rude Awakening

The canteen was a grimy building, filled with the labor crew. They all leaned against a counter that ran along the outside walls of the room. It must have been breaktime. The lack of tables and chairs discouraged the crew from lingering in the canteen for the whole shift. It looked like every person in the room was black except for the bleached-blond lady who worked the canteen. Several vending machines were lined against one wall, and there were guys pushing quarters into them for something quick to eat. The odor of stale tobacco mingled with the smell of over-brewed coffee.

As we entered, the crew took immediate notice of Sarge but didn't appear to notice me. "How's it goin', brotha?" said the first person we passed.

"What's shakin', Pop?" Sarge responded.

Pop had his own concession going on the island.

He roasted raw peanuts and chestnuts on top of the ovens he tended while he was working, and then he would sell them hot in small paper bags during breaks and lunch—great little hand warmers. And he was versatile—in warm weather, he sold cold pop from an ice chest he strapped to a hand truck he rolled to work every day from the parking lot. That's where he got his nickname, selling soda pop.

The greeting chant worked its way around until most of the men acknowledged him. Sometimes a nod or a grunt sufficed; sometimes they would bump fists or slap palms. I casually scanned the room but was being studiously ignored by everyone. I noticed a Latino man, who was ignoring Sarge and taking care of some personal business as money changed hands between him and two other workers.

"This is Johnnie's replacement," Sarge said finally. Johnnie apparently had been shot while robbing a liquor store and was recovering in the Wayne County General jail ward until his case came up. That's the way I heard it later anyway. I saw a few noncommittal nods, and then it got quiet. The underwhelming response made me feel self-conscious again. Besides the obvious, I was the only person in there with Levis on, not work pants or overalls. They felt stiff and tight because they were new and my thermal underwear was riding uncomfortably up my butt. I stood there like an idiot pulling at the back of my pants when someone finally acknowledged me.

"Who's your pet monkey, Sarge?" The sneering voice came from a light-skinned, freckle-faced young black guy with a reddish afro. There was little response from anyone until Sarge spoke up.

"Behave yourself, Lester."

I was already feeling awkward enough, being one of only a few white people there. Aside from me and the canteen manager, who was standing behind a small counter, there was a slightly built white guy who had just walked in. He worked without his bridgework, so they called him Smiley. The only way I knew he was white was from the pale circles around his eyes left by his goggles. The rest of his body was embedded with a charcoal residue.

This dusting was the great leveler on the island. Nobody on the island gave a damn who or what you were as long as you got your job done or figured some way to shut the operation down so everyone got paid for waiting around doing nothing until the end of the shift. Shutdowns created overtime.

Smiley was working a double shift and dragged himself to the counter. "How you doing, beautiful?" he said grinning a toothless smile at Helen, the canteen manager.

Wiping coffee from the countertop, she replied, "Fine, Smiley. What can I do you for?"

"Here you go, darling," he said handing her a crumpled slip of paper. "Here's my dinner voucher."

The company paid $2.75 in dinner money for

working a double shift. Helen wore a mechanical change counter to dispense quarters for the vending machines. In 1967, a dollar was still worth a little something. Since the voucher was paid in cash and tax free, many people pocketed the cash.

"You eatin' or cheatin' today, honey?"

"Lay the folding money on me today, babe. I need some gas to drive home."

She pulled a leather billfold from her apron, pulled out two dollars, and pushed the lever on her change dispenser three times.

"Thank you, darlin'," he said winking at her.

As he passed me to gather his work gear, he handed me the quarters in an unexpected gesture of generosity. "Here, kid. Never keep chump change. It'll burn you," he said pulling his goggles over his tired eyes. "Get yourself something warm to drink."

"Thanks." I didn't know at the time what he meant about the change until I worked in intense heat. Metal coins pick up and hold the heat; they can brand your leg through your pants pocket. It's a lesson quickly learned.

"Pulling another double, Smiley?" Sarge asked, but he already knew the answer.

"Yep! A dig out on Battery One. Another firewall caved in last night."

"Yeah, Scotty told me this morning. I need to rustle up some more guys. This is your third double this week. Don't work too hard!"

"There's no such thing, Sarge. I gots to make that bread!"

"Take it easy," I said trying to be friendly.

"I'll take it any way I can get it." With that, he walked out into the weather.

I took Smiley's advice and bought a cup of hot chocolate from a vending machine. The other men in the canteen ignored me until I heard another insulting remark from the same guy, "Who's your vanilla gorilla Sarge?"

"That's enough of that shit, Lester," Sarge shot back. "This young man has a bloodline here at Zug Island. So treat him with some respect!"

Evidently, Lester's reserves of "respect" were in short supply because he ignored his foreman. He was like a dog with a bone. "Do tell. A bloodline? Any colored blood in there? Mulatto maybe? Is that how you got this fine job?"

There was some nervous laughter and then an uneasy silence as if everyone was waiting for my reply. I wasn't sure what a mulatto was, but I got the gist of the remark. Ignoring his taunts, I took a gulp of scalding hot chocolate and blistered my tongue. I pulled the paper cup quickly from my mouth and spilled half of it down the front of my jacket. I said "Fuck!" reflexively and received some general laughter which seemed to ease the tension.

Sarge gave Lester a disgusted look, but he knew that I would have to make it on my own sooner or later. At home and in high school, I had a reputation for having a smart mouth, but this was an unfamiliar crowd, and my instincts cautioned against being too smart.

I ignored the race baiting. "Yeah ... some of my relatives worked here at one time or another. So it's my turn now."

Lester wasn't impressed. Eyeing my new shovel, he kept needling me. "I don't think I ever met Zug Island royalty before."

It was clear this guy wasn't going to let me be, so I took the bait. "That's probably because you're a self-made man." Several of the guys chuckled lightly. I'm not certain what I meant by that, but it was the first thing to come to my mind and out of my mouth. The affront was enough.

Lester was about to get in my face with his next insult when Sarge grabbed the shoulder of his jacket and pulled him towards the door. "You tired of working here, Lester?"

"What you talking about, man?"

"Time to get to work!" Sarge said pushing him out the door and into the weather. "Let's go, everybody. Report to your stations. Time to earn those paychecks."

The labor crew gravitated out the door. I tried to sip what was left of my hot chocolate, but it was still too hot, so I tossed it in the trash and followed the group to my first assignment.

The general laborers' primary task was to keep the conveyor belt catwalks and gangways clear of coke. Each belt spilled a predictable amount at every juncture where one belt transferred its load to another. The enclosed catwalks stretched like tentacles throughout much of the plant. The elevated tunnel structures had window openings at intervals for ventilation and natural light, but coke dust hung everywhere. Respirators were available, though most people didn't use them. I used one when the dust was unbearable, which was all too often.

As the crew paired off toward their work stations, I found myself once again walking with Sarge. We climbed ladders and catwalks to the upper reaches of the conveyor belt system; he pointed to a six-foot pile of coke mounting up on the floor beneath one of these belts. "Shovel this shit onto the belt to clear this catwalk. I'll check back on you later."

"How much later?"

"Lunchtime," he said. "Listen for the lunch whistle. Don't come looking for me; I'll come looking for you."

"Sounds good!"

"And don't let Lester harass you. He'll make you his personal nigger if you let him."

"Huh?" I was surprised by Sarge's use of the racial slur and thought I had heard him wrong.

"He's basically a coward. Just don't turn your back on him."

"Thanks for the advice," I replied. Sarge disappeared down the catwalk walking alongside the conveyor belt, his footfalls fading into the surrounding din.

I soon established a shoveling rhythm and quickly became impervious to the freezing weather. After a couple of hours, I had about half the pile cleared and decided to take a break. My arms, legs, and back were all limbered up, and I felt pretty good except for the blisters forming on my hands under my gloves. The cold wasn't bothering me, and even my ankle felt better.

I leaned out the ventilation window and looked across the Detroit River to Windsor. I took off my jacket and hardhat because I felt overheated. The sky was the brightest blue I had ever seen, and the background of sparkling snow on the frozen surface of the river was in stark contrast to the soiled snow around the plant. I wondered why Sarge had taken me to this remote station without another laborer for a partner, but I was just as happy to be working alone on my first day. Then, I heard that sneering voice again.

"There he is," Lester began his taunt turning to another black guy he had brought all the way up there to meet me.

I felt some panic all of the sudden. *Oh shit! I'm going to get killed, cut, or beat up at the very least.* I tried to remain calm. "Is it lunchtime yet?"

"You're a funny man, ain't ya, motherfucker?"

I didn't respond but shouldered my shovel as he angled towards me. The other guy hung back and watched impassively. I didn't know what to make of him, so I tried to keep one eye on each of them which was becoming harder and harder as Lester circled and edged towards me.

"Listen, you ofay motherfucker! I'm talking to you," he said, pointing for effect.

Again, I didn't know what to say. I wasn't sure what "ofay" meant, but paired with the other word I did know, I wasn't optimistic.

"Yeah, what do you want?" It was a question I really didn't want an answer for.

"What's a smart-assed white punk like you doing here?"

"Same as you. Working! You here to give me a hand shoveling this shit back on the belt?"

"Yeah, right, asshole!"

"What do you want from me?"

"I'll take that new shovel for starters. Then, I'm gonna whip your white ass with it, funnyman."

I knew if I let him bully me, I'd be eating his shit, or even worse, for as long as I worked there. He thought he had me cowering when I took him off balance.

"Me? No, I'm no funnyman. But you must be Lester the Jester if you think I'm going to hand this shovel over to you." I threw down the challenge. His buddy, smirking now, continued to lean against the wall. Emboldened, I continued, "You want something? Make your move, jerk face!"

"I'm gonna kick your ofay ass all the way back to

the suburbs." It was clear that my race was an issue with this fool. This was the first time I had been the object of racism, and I didn't care for it. Besides, it was obvious to me there was a redheaded Irishman somewhere in Lester's family tree, but I didn't hold that against him. He didn't come any closer. I had taken up a defensive position in an open area, so I could swing the shovel if I needed to.

"My white ass ... Now I know what you're here for. You're Lester the Molester." His sidekick laughed out loud. I'd won that round.

The frustrated Lester raised his clenched fists and continued circling me as I shifted with him. He cautiously measured me, so I knew he wasn't sure he could take me. "You gonna give me that shovel, or do I have to punch your pasty face in right now?"

I thought I could probably whip Lester, though the other guy worried me, but I knew there was no other way out. "You want to play baseball, ass-wipe? Take a swing!"

Instead of attacking me, this skinny idiot went for the shovel. We wrestled for it, and I knew I couldn't afford to let him take it from me. The wuss would probably club me with it. We jostled toward the center of the area to a large steel I-beam post that helped support the concrete top floor of this multistoried structure. After a brief struggle, I managed to maneuver Lester between the post and the shovel's long wooden handle. Shifting behind the post, I gripped the handle firmly with both hands and pulled back with my knee wedged behind the post and laid on the pressure to his chest. When he was about to pass out, I dropped him to the floor gasping for air. Good thing he went down. I was afraid I might have to whack him a good one with the shovel.

In the ruckus, I had forgotten about his friend who was still holding up the wall. "You want some?" I threatened, holding the shovel like a baseball bat.

"No, you earned that shovel," he said nodding. "Let's take a break. It's close enough to lunchtime."

"What?" I was taken off-balance. *Who is this guy? How is he connected with Lester? Where the hell is Sarge?* The entire morning had confused me. "Why should I trust you?" I asked.

"Who else is there?"

"Who the fuck are you?" I wasn't in the mood for any games.

"My name's Theo Semple. Get your lunchbox and I'll introduce you around."

I still wasn't sure about this guy. "What the hell are you doing here anyway?"

"Sarge sent me to look out for you. He paired me with Lester today."

"You mother … fuckers," came the labored voice from the floor.

"You be lookin' pretty sorry, Lester," Theo said grinning, revealing a gold tooth.

"Yeah, Lester the Loser," I said, adding insult to injury.

"Fuck you, white boy!"

"Want a face full of shovel, Poindexter?" I threatened holding it like a baseball bat and taking a step towards him. His hands instinctively shielded his head. I made another motion to swing the shovel, and he cowered again.

"Stay cool now! He's had enough. That right, Lester?"

"If you say so."

"Maybe you want some more?" I threatened again.

"No! No!"

"Give me any more shit, and you won't get off so easy next time." My bravado surprised even me.

Theo stepped up. "Stay here, Lester. You finish shoveling up this catwalk, or I'll tell everyone how you got your ass kicked by ... What's your name again?"

"Jake!" I said. "Jake Malone from ... Melvindale."

"Stay clear of my man from Melvindale. You hear me now?"

"Yeah, I hear you," Lester backpedaled. "I was just fooling around, man."

"Well, you picked the wrong fool," I said.

That was the last time I saw Lester. He didn't finish shoveling the catwalk, and I never heard about it from Sarge either. I wasn't sure about leaving my work station with Theo, but my elevated sense of confidence allowed me to lower my defenses. I took my shovel and lunch box and headed down the catwalk with Theo leaving Lester behind.

"You really from Melvindale?" Theo asked as we descended through the maze of conveyor belts and catwalks.

"Why would anyone lie about that?" I lied. This was getting ridiculous. It seemed like everything I did or said was being challenged at every turn. What disturbed me most was I suspected Theo knew I was lying.

"People lie for lots of reasons ... depending on the circumstances."

Great, I thought. *Another dumb fucking riddle.* "Like what?"

"If I had just whipped somebody's ass, I wouldn't be advertising my name and where I lived. That's either balls-out gutsy or just plain stupid."

He made a good point, but there was a third option he hadn't hit on. I was from Dearborn, whose mayor, Orville Hubbard, ran fifteen times undefeated and served thirty-six years straight. Hubbard was the poster child for Jim Crow segregation and anti-integration of the white suburban communities which surrounded the city of Detroit. His "Keep Dearborn Clean" campaign slogan was thinly disguised to mean "Keep Dearborn White." To obscure the obvious, the mayor had signs posted on every street entering the city, which read, "Keep Dearborn Clean. $100 fine for littering."

Dearborn was known and proud to be a "white only" town. It wasn't the only one, just the most blatant about it. Want to deny it? Look at any of the high school yearbooks from the era. The city was one of the most desirable areas in the Midwest to live. Dearborn could afford services other cities could only dream of. Most of the city's tax money came from the Ford Motor Company headquartered there. Blacks who tried to cross the real estate "red line" into Dearborn were discouraged by everything from threats and intimidation to the cutting off of city services and fire bombings. This was Mayor Orville Hubbard country. I was afraid I'd be marked lousy if it got out among the mostly black crew on the island, so I lied about it.

Growing up in Dearborn, I had great memories. We had lots of public parkland with neighborhood swimming pools, ice skating rinks, and toboggan runs which were all free to city residents. We had good, well-funded public schools, and a 626-acre rustic recreation area called Camp Dearborn north of town in rural Milford, Michigan, for Dearborn residents and their guests, if they were white.

It struck me that I had led a sheltered middle-class life there and was naïve and ignorant of the human condition only a handful of miles from my home. I needed to get some street smarts if I was going to survive here. The schoolboy routine wasn't going to get me very far. Theo could teach me a lot of what I needed to learn, so I decided to take a chance and trust him.

"Melvindale, huh?" he said, shaking his head from side to side. "It smells like rotten-egg farts over there."

"Yes, it does," I agreed. "But I live upwind of the natural gas plant,"

Another white lie, but I immediately felt guilty about it and came clean with him. "Hey, Theo? I'm from Dearborn."

"I know. Sarge told me."

Shit!

5
Breaking the Ice

W*alking with Theo towards* the canteen, I was still cautious and defensive. I'd known him for all of twenty-five minutes, under ambiguous circumstances at best. Then again, he spoke up for me at the end, when he and Lester could have jumped me and ruined my day. I wasn't sure what to do, but I knew I had to connect with someone soon, for self-preservation if nothing else. I calculated the risk as manageable and kept walking quietly.

Eventually, I broke the silence. "Sorry I lied to you back there. I didn't want any extra hassle." Walking in the open air made it easier for me to come clean with him. If he was pissed, I could keep heading to the parking lot and call it a day. I was looking for a job when I found this one. Maybe I could wash dishes in a Chinese restaurant or shovel snow for the neighbors.

"Who gives a shit? But take my advice—Jake Malone from Melvindale trips off the tongue. Stick with it while you're here."

Seemed like good advice to me.

Our break lapsed into lunch. I scarfed down my baloney and mayo sandwich, an apple, a pack of Twinkies, and a thermos of white milk in under ten minutes. Theo took his own sweet time and savored his lunch, something called porcupine balls, which he bought from a vending machine, along with a flimsy paper cup of hot black coffee that he sipped slowly. When he finished, he broke out a menthol cigarette and took great pleasure smoking it. These were solemn moments for him, almost thirty of them. He didn't talk much but concentrated on blowing smoke rings and watching them unravel and dissolve. I was antsy and ready to leave, but I took his lead and nursed the hot chocolate he bought me, especially after scalding myself with the one earlier that morning.

I waited for him to finish smoking. Finally, I couldn't stand it anymore. "How long do we get for lunch?"

"Depends."

"On what?"

"On the job you're doin'."

"What does that mean? I didn't finish the job I was supposed to do. Maybe we should get back."

Theo shrugged his shoulders, not overly concerned. "Don't burn yourself out on the first day."

"I'd hate to get fired."

"First day, last day … what's the difference?"

"That's easy for you to say, I—"

"Relax. Don't worry."

I grimaced and went over to the candy machine and bought myself a Snickers bar. I returned thinking I'd try to make some small talk to break the ice.

"Porcupine balls, huh?"

"Yeah, they're as tasty as they sound."

"What the hell are they, really?" I asked as he poked and prodded his food around the plate with a plastic fork.

"Fine dining, Jake. Ground pork and rice meatballs over egg noodles, smothered with brown gravy."

That was the extent of our conversation. Whenever someone came into the canteen and acknowledged him, he would glance over and nod without a large expense of words, so I didn't take it personally. We leaned against the counter for almost an hour. Boredom had set in, and I was getting edgy to leave. Just then, the foreman walked in bigger than shit.

"Hey!" Sarge nodded to us and shoved his gloves into his jacket pocket; then he went straight for a steaming cup of coffee and used it as a hand warmer.

That's it, I thought. My first day would be my last.

I quietly drank my hot chocolate and waited for my walking papers. Sarge lumbered over to us and stood next to me.

"How's your day going, Jake?"

"Good. No complaints." I wasn't sure if he knew about the ruckus with Lester, so I played it cool.

"Dirty enough for you?"

"About what I expected." I knew I must have been goggle-eyed by now. "Nothing I can't wash off," I said.

"Not like us. Right, Theo?"

"I guess not," he responded.

"I'm sorry," I backpedaled. "I didn't mean anything disrespectful by the remark." *Oh, shit! Here it comes now.*

"Well ... it'll wash off in about six months after you're done working here. Don't worry too much about it."

I felt like I had dodged a bullet.

"How far did you get with the dig this morning?"

"Over halfway maybe."

He looked down at the leading edge of my shovel and saw that it was worn about a half inch. "Don't work yourself out of a job, Jake. Pace yourself."

"I was just tellin' him that, Sarge."

Sarge turned and spoke to Theo, "Give this young man the ten-cent tour, but make sure you guys clear out the rest of that area before the shift ends. A welding crew is scheduled to make some repairs up there tonight."

"No problem, Sarge," I responded with a sudden show of initiative.

Theo simply nodded as we put on our gloves and headed out. Not a word about the shovel scuffle or where Lester was. I felt great. My day was improving, and the cold wind didn't bite like it had before. Either I was getting used to it, or hypothermia had set in.

We slung our shovels over our shoulders and walked back towards the coke ovens. I tried to strike up a conversation with Theo. "I'm excited about this!"

"About what?"

"The tour. I love plant tours. Ever been on the Rouge Plant tour?"

"The what?"

"The Rouge Plant. The big-assed Ford plant just up the Rouge River from us. Raw materials go in one end; finished cars come out the other."

"No shit."

"How long have you lived around here?" I couldn't believe he had never heard of the Rouge Plant. It was world-famous and only a couple of miles away.

"Goin' on two years."

I was determined to draw him out and make conversation. "Where are you from, Theo?" He hadn't said much, so I couldn't identify his accent beyond his black dialect. I knew he wasn't from around here, though.

"You're a chatty bastard, ain't ya?" he replied.

"I'm just curious ... I appreciate you helping me out back there." I thought thanking him would put him at ease with me. Just barely. "You're not a Detroiter, are you?"

"No, I'm from down South."

"That narrows it down," I quipped. "Where down South?"

"Memphis. You know where that is?"

"Memphis, Tennessee? Sure, I have relatives who live just outside of Nashville. Ever been to the Grand Ole Opry?"

He looked at me with disbelief. "Not really. That's white people's music."

It struck me that other than Charlie Pride, who sung like a white man, there were no blacks in country and western music. Again, I realized I was way out of my element.

"I took a sweaty bus ride through Nashville on my way to Detroit."

"When I was a kid, my father took us on a couple of car trips down there. My mother was born there, so I guess that gives me Southern roots."

"Guess so."

That conversation died an early death, and it became silent again except for the infernal plant racket which I hadn't learned to ignore yet.

Zug Island was full of people from the South doing

the nasty work that many white Detroiters wouldn't do, namely foundry, blast furnace, and coke oven work. Theo wasn't the only transplant. Many Southerners of both races came north to work in Detroit's heavy industry during the war years and long after. Some migrated permanently in and around the Detroit area.

Others commuted home monthly. Seemed like a long way to go for a job to me, but by working double shifts and living in cheap residential hotels for nearly a month on end, many of these men took their five-day break for working a swing shift and carpooled back home once a month, with a fresh haircut, a clean shave, and a pocketful of money. To hear them tell it, they lived like kings back home because the cost of living was so much lower in the South, and wages were rock-bottom there if you could find a job.

The swing shift appealed to many of these workers. They'd put in a week of days and get two days off, then a week of afternoons with two days off, and finally a week of midnights with five days off. Being away from home most of the month seemed like a high price to pay, but what did I know? I lived at home rent free. Some of these guys had girlfriends in Detroit and a wife and family back home. To each his own.

I attempted to pick up the thread of my earlier

conversation with Theo. "You ought to take the tour sometime."

"To Nashville?"

"No! The Rouge Plant tour."

"Why?"

"It's interesting, that's all."

"I should do that?"

"Yeah! Why not?"

"On my day off?"

"Sure, it would be fun."

"Fun? After spending eight to sixteen hours a day here, a factory is the last fuckin' place I want to be on my day off," he spoke up. "Fun! You call that fun? Chasing women and playin' cards is fun. How fuckin' old are you, anyway?"

"Fine, I'm just trying to make conversation." I was all set to tell him about the Corn Flake tour at the Kellogg plant in Battle Creek, but to hell with him. I walked along silently, so I wouldn't agitate him further. I was truly looking forward to more of the Zug Island tour. The plant was a giant clockwork where I could lose myself and mark time.

The shoveling end of this operation, I already had down. It wasn't all that different from shoveling snow after a blizzard. *There are obvious differences, of course,* I thought as I allowed my mind to wander. *Snow is white; coke is black. One is soft; the other is hard. One is born of water; the other of fire. But they both have a habit of piling up, getting in the way, and clogging up the works. It's the same scrape and toss though.* The repetitive motion seemed to have a calming effect on me.

Just before we got to the ovens, we stopped at a fifty-five gallon barrel full of blazing planks torn from shipping pallets mixed in with chunks of blazing coke. Two old-timers were roasting large sausages skewered on lengths of narrow steel rods. The fat sizzled and popped, giving off the unmistakable aroma of roast sausage, making my mouth water.

"Smells heavenly, Brother Williams," Theo said, warming his hands before the fire.

"Want a taste, Theo?"

"Don't mind if I do."

With one hand, the man reached into a makeshift bun-warming box next to the blazing steel drum and pulled out a steaming bun. With the other hand, he sliced the bun open with a long knife in a single motion and eased one of the impaled sausages off the skewer into the warm bun. He was practiced at this.

"There you go, Theo. Reach into that paper bag for some condiments," said Brother Williams. "How about your buddy?"

"Jake, you want some donkey dick?"

There was a fixation on food named after animals' genitalia on Zug Island; I couldn't get the image out of my mind. "No, I think I'll pass. Thanks anyway."

"Brother Williams, Smokin' Joe, meet Jake Malone from Melvindale."

"Pleased to meet you, gentlemen," I said.

"Right back at you, son," Smokin' Joe said giving me an encouraging nod.

To make some small talk, I asked, "Did you take your name from Smoking Joe Frazier?"

Theo's eyes rolled up into his head.

"No, son," the grey-bearded old gentleman laughed. "I was the first."

It struck me how stupid my question was, but Smoking Joe was good-natured about it.

"Nice to make your acquaintance, son," Brother Williams said thrusting his hand forward to shake hands. I guessed I was destined to be everyone's son. I had better get used to it.

"Thank you, sir."

"Call me Brother Williams," he smiled. "Sir doesn't sit too well on me. I prefer my Christian name."

"Brother Williams," I said with a change of heart, "that sausage is smelling mighty good. Can I have a taste?"

"Don't burn your mouth on it, son," he cautioned.

"Too late! The hot chocolate I drank this morning did that." The blistered sausage casing cracked, oozing clear running juices down my chin as I nibbled at the end. "Um-um! This is the best sausage I ever ate!" I made two instant friends that day as the cooks smiled with approval.

"If you've got a sweet tooth that needs feeding, we've got some marshmallows and graham crackers in the sack."

"Thanks," said Theo finishing up his sausage roll. "Maybe next time, I've got to finish showing Jake around the plant."

"Catch you later," I said, walking off. "Thanks for the sausage. Man, this tastes good."

We headed towards the wharf area and saw a billowing steam cloud rise from the quenching station. The huge icicles hanging about the station glinted water diamonds in the bright sunshine. Walking past them earlier in the morning darkness had given no hint of their dazzling beauty. Such are the contrasts between hot and cold, light and dark, day and night.

"Wow! Those icicles are spectacular," I remarked.

"You get used to 'em," Theo said unimpressed.

After quenching its load, the hot car raced back to the wharf and dropped it onto the sloped fire brick surface. I had seen this operation from above and was happy to see it from ground level. The steaming coke slid down to a system of heavy gates that kept it from rushing all at once onto the conveyor belt below. It was the wharf man's job to lift each gate, allowing a manageable amount onto the belt.

Theo pointed at the ovens. "That's where the coke comes from and that's where it goes," he said pointing to the wharf, demonstrating he had a firm grasp of the obvious. It was apparent that Sarge had a better handle on the operation than Theo had.

"Fascinating. I went over this with Sarge this morning," I said following him down some half-dozen worn, concrete steps into the realm of the wharf man. He was at the far end pulling a gate open. There were about twenty of these gates. This job required strength, control, and judgment.

"That's Bull," Theo said with a nod.

I wasn't certain what he meant. Either the job was lousy or it was the man's name. Rather than ask, I thought I'd listen for a change and wait to find out. I was starting to learn.

The old man was short and stout with shoulders like an ox, and his hands and face were heavily wrinkled. He was working with his jacket open, sweating profusely from huge pores on his weathered face. He had to be close to seventy years old if he was a day.

"What's up, Chief?"

"New man?" he asked looking over at me.

"Bull Rider, this is Jake Malone ... from Melvindale."

Names were often colorful on the island, but what the hell kind of name was Bull Rider? A nickname ... I had no idea. I was tiring of being introduced as "Jake Malone from Melvindale." It sounded dorky. Maybe they'd start calling me Melvin; I decided that I liked "son" better, but not much. Nicknames seemed to work at Zug. "Pleased to meet you," I said, holding out my hand to him. His calloused, vise grip of a hand squeezed the water blisters on my palm and hurt like hell.

"You here to spell me, Theo?" Bull asked as he

unzipped his pants and relieved himself on the empty, moving conveyor belt.

"Yeah, no problem."

"I'll see you in about twenty minutes," he said with a quick zip and vanished up the steps.

"Let's pull some gates, Jake."

"Aren't we supposed to be on a tour?"

"Forget about that for right now. This is part of your training!"

The hot car returned and dumped another load. The hot car operator saw Theo leaning against one of the gates and yelled down to him, "You ever gonna spell me you lazy son of a bitch?" Theo gave him a noncommittal shrug.

"Watch me!" he said, slowly pulling a gate open. "The trick is not letting too much of this shit onto the belt at once. Too much and somebody has to shovel it when it falls off down the line. That would be you."

"I can relate to that."

"Think you can handle it?"

"Sure, looks easy enough."

"We'll see. If you don't put enough of this shit on the belt, you'll be pulling gates nonstop all day tryin' to keep up with the hot car, feeding the blast furnaces, and loading them train cars."

"Christ, how difficult could it be?" I gave a tug but the gate didn't budge. I put my full weight into the next pull and a landslide of coke tumbled onto and off the belt. It was a disaster. I hoped Theo would rush over and snatch the gate from me. But no such luck! My hands ached and my upper body muscles strained to close the gate.

"Ease it open this time." He didn't give a shit if I was doing it right or not. He went to the far end of the wharf and hiked himself onto the guardrail with his back to the work. "Don't worry. You'll get the hang of it." He lit a hand-rolled cigarette and inhaled deeply. "Want a hit?"

"No, I don't smoke," I said struggling with the gates.

"Good boy," he chuckled.

The hot car returned and dropped another load. The wharf was backing up with coke. The hot car operator squinted at the unfamiliar person struggling with the gates; he reached into the cab and put on a pair of glasses. "Who the hell are you?" he shouted.

"Jake Malone, from Melvindale," I yelled back.

With a salute, he said with a Southern accent, "Welcome aboard!" Then he turned his attention to Theo. "Hey, you peckerwood. Are you the spell man today or what, motherfucker?"

Theo didn't bother to turn around. He took a long draw on his smoke and with his free hand simply gave him the finger.

"I need a goddamn break here pretty soon," the hot car operator shouted, "I'm about to shit my pants, you lazy bastard."

"They're your pants," Theo replied unconcerned.

"Well, when then?"

Slightly turning his head, he said, "When Bull gets back."

"Fucking great!" the hot car operator said as he sped to catch another waiting load.

"Who's he?" I asked.

"A dumb-assed hillbilly from Bumfuck, Kentucky. He used to work on the ore boats once, so we call him the admiral. He's an asshole."

"What's a spell man?" I asked wrestling to control the gates.

Exhaling another drag, he was about to explain the obvious to me again when his eyes widened, and he rushed to a hose along the back wall. "Close that fuckin' gate!"

"Why? What's wrong?" I asked barely managing to shut it.

"Some glowing coke fell onto the conveyor belt," he said, hitting a kill switch to stop the belt. "Quick—douse that hot spot with this hose before it burns through the rubber belt."

"Shit! Now what's gonna happen?"

"If it's hot enough, it could burn through the belt. Then the whole operation could shut down and someone loses his job."

"Really? How many more ways can I find to get fired today?"

"Not this time. We caught it early enough. That's another part of this job—fire tender."

"What's your job?"

"Spell man. I rotate and give people in key jobs a break."

"You must be behind, according to the admiral."

"The admiral can wait to whack off. Fuck him if he can't take a joke."

The water blisters on my palms had burst, and my bladder was brimming. "You mind taking over for a bit? I need to go to the bathroom."

"The bathroom? You go to the restroom, the shower room, or the shithouse. Never the bathroom! Piss on the belt like everyone else does." He was finished smoking, and his practiced hands wrestled the gates open clearing the wharf in short order.

While relieving myself, I asked, "What kind of name is Bull Rider?"

"Fuck, I don't know. It's what we call him."

"Is it his real name or a nickname?"

"What's the difference? It's what he goes by."

"It's my real name now, son," came a gruff voice from behind me.

Startled, I fumbled with an apology. "Sorry, I meant no disrespect."

"None taken, son. It's the nickname I picked up on the rodeo circuit when I was about your age, another lifetime ago."

"The rodeo, huh. That's great!"

"Yeah, it was for a while. I rode Brahmin bulls out West. That's how I got my name."

"How'd you get into riding bulls?"

"Jake, anyone ever tell you that you ask too many questions?" Theo warned.

"How am I going to find out stuff unless I ask?"

"You writing a book for Christ's sake? Leave the man alone."

"I don't mind," Bull said. Pulling gates is a solitary job, and I think he wanted to talk. "It was a way to get off the rez."

"The what?" There were no limits to my ignorance.

"The Indian reservation in Oklahoma."

"Really? That's incredible!"

"Hey, Chief, why don't you tell him your life story next time? I need to spell the admiral before he craps his pants. We'll catch you in the funny papers."

"I'd like to talk more with you sometime. Can I call you Chief?"

"Call me Bull, son."

The hot car was our next stop. The admiral jumped out of his cab cursing like a sailor. Going back and forth on a straight set of rails must have been a letdown for him after cruising the Great Lakes on a freighter. Theo and I barely fit inside, but I managed to squeeze in. The hot car was electrically controlled by a simple lever. Left was forwards; right was backwards; the center was dead stick.

Watching tons of blazing coke collapse into the

hot car as we drove slowly towards it was spectacular, second only to the tapping of a blast furnace. After Theo caught a couple of loads, I wanted to try my hand at it.

"You need to be specially trained for this job."

"You didn't have a problem with me pulling those damned gates," I reminded him. "My hands are raw from that."

"Forget about it!"

"How tough can it be?"

"Cause I can do it?"

"No, that's not what I meant.

"Like them gates? Guess who's gonna dig that fucker out in the morning?"

It had to be me.

"You could run this car into the end of the quenching station or cremate us both. I can wait for the everlasting bonfire."

"I'll take it easy."

"Learn to take no for an answer. You don't want to get too smart too fast around here."

"All right then."

"You need training and clearance to work this job. It's a union rule. The job pays more."

"I'll work for less!"

"Sorry."

"Who'll know?" I persisted.

"You want me to get in trouble with the union? You're one crazy son of a bitch."

We rode along quietly and caught another load before I spoke again. "Seeing as I'm just along for the ride, tell me something."

"What?"

"Tell me why Sarge sent you over with Lester this morning?"

Theo pursed his lips. "Ain't it obvious?"

"How about an answer before another question? What'd he tell you?"

"To shadow your sorry ass. He knew Lester would seek you out and start some shit."

"So he sent you to protect me?" I said offended.

"Humiliating, ain't it?" he smiled.

"You scared the hell out of me. I didn't know if I was going to have to fight both of you or what. I'm still half expecting Lester to jump out and slam me with the butt end of my own shovel."

"He's out of here by now."

"Oh, yeah? Why are you so sure of that?"

"He was about to get fired anyway. All he's done since he's been here is cause problems."

"Like what?"

"You should know. He's a trash-talking thief. Everyone suspects him of rippin' off stuff out of the locker room. He's always fuckin' with people too."

"Why didn't you step in and break up the scuffle before it got started?"

"Because Lester needed an ass kicking, and you needed to prove yourself," he said making no apologies. "Besides, it was funny! I thought his peanut head was going to pop like a blood blister when you pinned him against that beam."

"I'm glad I could cheer you up."

"There's something else."

I thought I knew what was coming next. "What?"

"Sarge wants me to find out your story. The rest of us have to put up with this nasty-assed place; we don't have much of a choice. No offense, but it don't add up."

"What are you guys? A bunch of mathematicians? I already told him. I was tossed out of college for drinking. Big deal! That's it. End of story!"

"Like that's gonna satisfy him."

We raced to the next oven and another load fell into the hot car. While it was quenching, I decided to come out with it. It was clear to me that I'd be hounded until I did. "The whole thing was pretty embarrassing. I'm trying hard to put it behind me and forget about it."

"How bad can it be?" For a guy who hadn't said much all day, Theo was making up for it now. "What's the story?"

"It sounds stupid to tell it, but I was innocent. I got caught up in the bullshit of the place and now I'm here."

"If you were drinking, how were you innocent?"

"It's a long boring story." I was feeling really cramped, and I hoped the admiral's shore leave would end soon. "A half-truth is hard to defend yourself against."

"Give me the goddamned details; we don't have all day." He was worse than a gossipy old crone.

"The guys in the adjoining dorm room had partied there, and one of the jerks tossed a wastebasket full of empties out of the fourth floor window near the dorm manager's ground-floor apartment. The racket woke him up, so he checked it out."

"Well, where do you come in?"

"The guys in the adjoining room left at about eleven o'clock to buy more beer. The dorm manager saw the fourth floor window open, called the campus police, and used his passkey to enter our room. They found me and my roommate sleeping it off in our beds. We had been off campus, drinking with friends in an apartment. The cops turned in a report without looking into it further, and we got busted. End of story."

"So the dorm manager put two and two together and got five."

"No, he put two and two together and got two. Me and my buddy! We got blamed for what the other guys did. And I didn't squeal on the assholes, thinking they would feel guilty and come forward."

"I'll be damned, but you're right. It does sound pretty stupid," Theo said shaking his head.

"Right! I overestimated human nature and paid the price."

"Don't do that again!"

"What's taking the admiral so long?" I complained.

"He's gettin' back at me for making him wait. I hope that asshole is in the shower room washing the shit out of his drawers."

We laughed at the prospect.

"So you didn't rat them out?"

"No. I'm not a snitch. Not very smart, huh?"

"You're a real piece of work. You'll fight over a stupid shovel but take getting thrown out of college in stride. That's strange."

"What else could I do? I packed up my stuff and moved back home. The damage had been done. Why complicate matters?"

Theo wasn't as passive as I had originally thought; he was a cagey character. "That's a crying shame," he said shaking his head again. "But why work here? This place is as nasty as it gets."

"After getting screwed over in college, I wanted to surround myself with a better class of people."

He chortled.

"I'm glad you find my misery entertaining."

"You were just having a bad day. You didn't wimp out like those other shit-faced punks. Just like this morning—you didn't back down from Lester. You're a stand-up guy, Jake. I respect that."

That's what I needed to hear. It made me feel a twinge of pride.

"About fuckin' time!" Theo told the admiral as he

slowly approached. "I was worried you had ripped your dick off."

"Yeah, if that ever happens, I'll save it for your lunch. Kid, don't take any shit from this idiot!"

"Thanks for the advice," I said giving him a mock salute. To my surprise, he returned it.

"Carry on," he said.

We left the battery and headed up the catwalk to shovel out the rest of the morning's dig. Teaming up with Theo made it easier for me to settle into the job. He was easygoing and liked by almost everyone. He never made demands on anyone. He went with the flow, even though he might get turned around every once in awhile; as long as he was floating, he was content. He taught me a lot that day.

When I went to the canteen at the end of the shift to get my lunchbox, it was gone. I didn't give a shit about the lunchbox, but my father's thermos was in there. Another hard lesson learned.

6 *Crossing the River Styx*

S*ix weeks passed without* incident, and I was still driving my mom's rickety, two-door hardtop, '63 Rambler American, a proud product of the American Motor Corporation. It was a red, rusted-out piece of junk with two sad eyes for headlights and a grille that frowned. Under the hood was an inline-six engine that whined out a whopping 125 HP. My dad's brother, my sympathetic uncle Patrick, gave it to my mother when I needed a car for work, and she lent it to me. My mother had never driven the car, but the fact that it was hers made it clear I was dependent on her for the privilege.

Until my father died, my mom had never applied for a driver's license because she was "just a housewife" and didn't have a job. If she absolutely needed to be somewhere, she either got a lift from nearby family members or she took a taxi in a pinch. My mother was forty-two when she got her first license. She seldom drove the '65 Buick LeSabre my father had died in. The LeSabre, besides being newer and in better condition, was built like a tank, which made my mother feel safer on the roads. The Rambler I drove handled like a breadbox and smelled like a hamper of unwashed underwear. Knowing my uncle as I did, I could only guess what he was doing in that car. At least the cold weather kept the stale, musty smell in check. What can I say, it was a crummy car that saw a lot of action!

My mother didn't trust me with the LeSabre's 300-cubic-inch V-8, with the Powerglide automatic tranny that cranked out 250 HP, and I can't say I blamed her much as things currently stood with us. More often than not, she would wait for me to get home to drive her places, with the proviso that on special occasions I might be able to borrow the LeSabre in the future.

Starting the Rambler in cold weather was always an act of faith. It would groan and stutter several times before it sputtered to life; then, it would shake so much that the rearview mirror rattled. Once the car warmed up, the defrosters could clear only enough of the windshield to make the damned thing drivable, a spot the size of a flattened softball. The three-speed shifter on the column was sticky in reverse and ragged in second gear. It was a thrill ride every time I got behind the wheel.

I was running late for the midnight shift one miserable February evening, driving as fast as my slipping tires and the pavement would allow. My right front tire dropped into a deep pothole on West Jefferson just past the Rouge River Bridge. The tie-rod snapped, and my wheel folded under the weight of the car. It jerked right and slid through the frozen curb slush between a fire hydrant and a telephone pole. All things considered, I lucked out. It could have been much worse.

Now what? I asked myself. I got out, walked around the front end and assessed the damage. If the car had been a horse, I would have shot it on the spot to put it out of its misery. I gave the bastard a swift kick in the grille and cursed my luck. At least the broken-down heap was off the street. It was 11:37 PM and I was less than a mile from the plant entrance, so I grabbed my work gear and abandoned the car. I'd deal with it tomorrow, but I hoped that it might somehow disappear before morning and never be heard from again. I'd be late for my shift, but I wasn't working a key job, so it wouldn't be critical. At least I showed up for work every day; that's more than some of my coworkers could say.

Walking through Delray at midnight was not my idea of a good time. At almost midnight, the frigid howling winds and blowing snow made the deserted street feel like a scene from a cheap film noir classic.

I focused on my transportation situation to get my mind off my late-night stroll through skid row. I hated that broken-down heap and needed a reliable car. My mom was afraid that if I bought a car my college days would be over. But it wasn't like I was wild in the streets or some raving lunatic. I was planning to commute the thirty miles to Ypsilanti with Mark anyway; we would take turns carpooling. Living on campus hadn't worked for me, so I thought I would try being a freeway flyer to see how that worked.

Yeah! That's how I'd pitch it to my mom. She had made me agree that most of the money I earned would go towards a college fund, or else I'd have to pay her room and board. Not a bad deal in the abstract, but I needed some wheels on the concrete. By working all the double shifts I could, I had already saved over four hundred dollars beyond the school money. I could use that for a down payment. *Yeah, that'll work,* I thought.

Musing over what I could afford, a pair of misaligned headlights approached me from behind with the horn blaring. I looked over my shoulder and prepared to jump out of the way; then I noticed it was Theo in his rusted-out '61 Chrysler Imperial. It skidded to a stop. I looked through the cracked windshield and saw his grinning face. The right front power window groaned down. "What's happenin', Jake?"

"I thought I'd walk to work to get some fucking exercise, until you scared the shit out of me."

"I saw your car back there. Some fancy drivin'. Just missed the pole."

"And the fire hydrant."

"Hop in!"

I tried the door handle but it was broken.

"Hop in through the window for Christ's sake. The door is wired shut."

I lowered myself into his car, boots first, and then shimmied into the front passenger seat. "Thanks. I'm freezing my balls off out there."

"Yeah, I brought my brass monkey in last night. Try some of this." He held out a paper bag with a pint of Mohawk sloe gin inside. "A slug or two of this will warm you up."

I hadn't drunk anything since my college debacle, but I took a couple of sips to be social. I didn't care for it. "Thanks," I said returning the pint. He took a gulp, capped it, and slipped the bottle into his pocket.

"Gonna work another double today?"

"If I can, I will. I've got to buy me a car."

"How many doubles have we worked in the last two weeks?

"Three or four ... I forget."

"All work and no play. No fun, no way." He got the cliché half right.

"Why not work as much as I can? Time and a half adds up."

"Yes it does, but all we do is work and sleep."

"Most of my friends are away at college or in the service, so I don't mind working."

"You need to do some living now. You almost ate it on the bridge tonight, my man."

Suddenly, he steered his car hard to the right and fishtailed into the back entrance of the island, throwing me left and right along the bench seat. "Jesus Christ! What the hell are you doing?"

"Quit crying, old lady." He laughed.

I didn't know where the back entrance to the island was because it was an unmarked train trestle obscured by years of overgrowth. Even in winter, it was hidden with tangled brush and vines. This bridge was barely the width of a train track and open only during the midnight shift and early in the day shift to help get the work force onto the island. Otherwise, the bridge was only for train traffic. Theo raced to the parking lot and skidded hard into a space. We both got out on the driver's side and walked to the clock house with two minutes to spare.

As we clocked in, he asked what I was going to do about the Rambler.

"I'll get it towed when the shift ends," I answered. "I've got Triple-A road service."

"Got any plans for the long weekend?"

"Yeah! Buy a car. Finance one, anyway." I paused. "That's if my mom goes for it."

"It's your money, ain't it?"

"Well, it's not that cut-and-dried," I answered. "She will have to cosign the loan."

"Listen, momma's boy! How are you supposed to get to work? Walk?"

"Ouch!" I reacted to his taunt. "First, I need to convince my mom that it's in everyone's best interest. I'll suggest I drive her Buick first, but that will leave her without transportation. The only places she goes are shopping, church, and bingo once a week, but my swing shift would interfere with her schedule."

"Bingo?"

"Yeah, at the Knights of Columbus Hall."

"The what?"

I wasn't in the mood to explain the Catholic fraternal order or the sacrament of bingo to him. "Forget that! I need to think this car thing through."

"Hell, it's easy to buy a car. All you need is a down payment and a job. They'll be happy to let you drive out of the showroom with anything you want."

"We'll see."

"No problem." Theo was more convinced than I was, but I had seen the bag of bolts he was driving, so I wasn't as confident.

"When you get your new car, we need to go on a power cruise someplace together."

After a slight beat, I said, "Sure." This was the first time he had talked about doing something outside of work, and I balked. I felt terrible about it too. I didn't think of myself as prejudiced, especially when held up to the mirror of my community's conservative, openly racist attitudes, including those of both branches of my own family. Compared to them, I was a liberal. Anybody who socialized with blacks was a "nigger lover" in their eyes.

I had never socialized with a colored person, or ever spoken to one in person before I started working at the mill, not by choice as much as lack of exposure. There was an invisible red line that ran between Detroit and the white suburban communities bordering it. Dearborn wasn't the only city, just the most notorious.

Entrenched discrimination was respected and protected by realtors and openly understood by white buyers and sellers. The unwritten law was you never sold your home to colored people; they would bring down the property values. If a black family dared move into a white community, the family was intimidated or burned out. The neighbors could always be counted on to have heard or seen nothing. I grew up with these attitudes unchallenged, but even as a kid I knew they were wrong.

The roots of racism run deep and dark in the Detroit area, shaped and aggravated by the automobile industry through its manipulation of the labor movement. The Ford Motor Company wasn't the only auto manufacturer that practiced racism, but Ford was the area's largest employer and had the greatest impact on the local economy.

Early in the company's history, Henry Ford deliberately hired European immigrants from conflicting ethnic groups who had longstanding hatreds and suspicions. At first, their cultures and languages clashed, which made it hard for them to organize a union. But by the 1930s, the workers wised up and put their ethnic differences aside for the common good and organized the United Auto Workers. Then, Ford began to hire blacks from the South to capitalize on racial division and hatred, pitting whites against blacks. Despite their differences or foreign accents, these white people had one common bond—they hated black people. Henry Ford's attempt to divide his labor force left the city with a festering legacy of racial division and hatred.

After World War II, there was white flight from Detroit to the ever-expanding suburbs. Most white adults thought of the inner city as a large cauldron where blacks and mixed-race couples could stew in their own juices.

Blacks didn't live in my town, go to my school, or attend my church. In fact, the only black people I was exposed to as a child were celebrities on television like Sammy Davis Jr., Pearl Bailey, Nat King Cole, and Ella Fitzgerald. Each had a carefully constructed, homogenized media image to make him or her less threatening to white audiences. Black entertainers who acted white and played the game were marginally accepted by white America. These performers, considered integration pioneers, opened doors for blacks of later generations, as black entertainers before their time opened doors for them, like the Depression-era Bill "Bo Jangles" Robinson in the Shirley Temple movies my mother loved and forced us to watch as children, and the serious dramatic actor, Paul Robeson, who commanded respect on and off the silver screen.

My main impression of black people was from movies where they played either servants, slaves, or natives in Tarzan movies. Even in the affable *Charlie Chan in Egypt* movie, comic actor Stepin Fetchit gives a stereotypical performance that was over-the-top even in those days. But I'd learned some respect and admiration for blacks, like so many white kids of my generation had. As a teen, I snuck down into the basement and wore the grooves smooth on my Motown and Chess record collection: Smokey Robinson and the Miracles, the Supremes, the Temptations, Aretha Franklin, the Four Tops, Jackie Wilson, Chuck Berry, and Little Richard. "Good Golly, Miss Molly!"

The pop-radio playlist of black music was endless and continues to dominate America's rhythm and blues and pop-music songbooks today. Somehow, Pat Boone in a cardigan sweater singing "Tootie Fruity" paled by comparison; when he covered Fats Domino's "Blueberry Hill," he sold millions of copies, aided by the white music establishment. This was when Motown and other black labels didn't show their Negro artists on their album covers, so white kids could sneak the records into the house.

In theory, I had no problem with integration; in practice, it troubled me. I felt guilty, but I answered the only way my conscience would allow. "Sure, we'll go somewhere. How about downtown?" I knew that no one I knew was likely to see me there.

While I struggled with my moral dilemma, Theo had more practical concerns. "What kind of car do you want?"

"I'm not sure. I just started seriously thinking about it."

"How does a ruby red Continental with power everything, leather interior, and an eight-track stereo sound to you? That's my dream car."

"You couldn't afford the gas."

"Don't I know it." He laughed. "What's your dream car, Jake?"

"In my world of wants, I'd like a midnight blue, hardtop convertible Thunderbird." Then, I came back to reality. "But I'll get something I can afford, like a Falcon."

"At least you're consistent," Theo noted.

"I don't get it. How?"

"Both cars you mentioned have the names of birds."

I thought for a second until it made some kind of

sense to me. Technically, the Thunderbird was a trademark and not a real bird. I let it pass.

"I think it's ironic we both want Ford products." It was his turn to be perplexed.

"Why?"

"Because of the history of this town."

"I don't know nothin' about Detroit history. Just don't be showing up in a Falcon, or a Corvair, or a Dart or some other tinny-assed piece of shit like that."

"It won't be a Rambler. That's for sure! Maybe I'll buy something used."

With a sly grin and a gleam in his eyes, he said, "I've got an Imperial for sale."

"Really? Why don't you drive it off the Ambassador Bridge and put it out of its misery?"

"I can't," he said, frowning. "The bank still holds the pink slip on it."

"Then we both better keep working doubles, bro'."

"Amen to that."

7 Changing of the Guard

When we arrived at the battery, Theo was scheduled to be spell man as usual, and I was assigned to be tar chaser. Tar chaser was the easiest job at the plant. Huge stand pipes draw off gases and tar from the tops of the ovens and route them to the by-products plant. During the summer, the tar flows without much coaxing, but in the winter, the subfreezing temperatures thicken the tar into stiff goo that needs to be softened and moved along. If the pipe clogged, pressure would build up and an explosion could occur.

Every so often along the top of the pipe, there was an access hole covered by a tar-caked cap. The tar chaser took a steam wand with an off/on lever to control the pressure and inserted it periodically into the holes to soften, stir, and coax the tar through the pipe. If this was done along the length of the pipe every half hour or so, the pressure readings in the control room stayed within reasonable limits. Normally, because this station was so out of the way from the coke battery, no one ever checked on me up there, so it was a good place to catch up on sleep. I was picking up some of my mentor's bad habits.

I brought a windup clock from home and reset the alarm at thirty-minute intervals. I napped when I could and chased tar the rest of the time. A long shed enclosed the stand pipe and gave some protection from the weather. Heat radiating from the pipe made it warm and cozy in there. I took out my transistor pocket radio and listened to the top forty on CKLW.

At almost 3:30 AM, the door opened and Theo blew in. "What's goin' down, Jake?"

"Just kicking back," I said sitting up from an uncomfortable crouch. "I was almost asleep until you barged in."

"Well, get off your dead ass and spell me for awhile," Theo said.

My alarm was about to go off anyway, so I pushed in the off switch on the back and started wrestling with the steam hose, dragging it from one opening to the next, stirring up the coal tar.

The pint came out of Theo's work coat. "Have some?"

"Naw, I've had enough .... It makes me groggy."

"Me too!" he said gulping down the last few swallows. "Don't let me sleep past daybreak," he said adjusting himself on my wooden bench leaning against the shed. He propped his feet up on a steel barrel. His rubbery spine seemed to fit into any position for maximum comfort. There was no wasted motion in anything he did.

"Comfy?"

"It'll do for now."

"I'm so glad."

What nerve! I thought. He cons me into doing his job while he sleeps. Sweet deal for him! I decided not to be a pushover, so I gave him some shit. "Daybreak is over two hours away, asshole!"

"I know," he answered with his hardhat tipped over his eyes. "How about spellin' the chief for me?"

"You must be fucking nuts. No way! Why would I want to do that?"

Undeterred, he continued, "When you're finished with that, spell the admiral also."

That was the one job I wanted to do, but I didn't want to jump too fast at it. "What about the union?"

"Fuck the union! It's the midnight shift."

"And while I'm doing that, what are you gonna do?"

"Set the alarm for 5:00, and I'll give the pot a good stir then."

A change of scenery always made the shift seem shorter, but I wasn't through messing with him yet. I set the clock for 3:55 AM, which was only ten minutes away. He'd just be dozing when it went off. I gave the windup clock a couple of quick turns, smiled to myself, and placed it beyond his reach.

"Who's gonna give me clearance on the hot car? The admiral won't."

"You rotate the lever back and forth?"

"What about braking?"

"Dead stick the motherfucker! It's like running a toy train."

"I don't know …"

"Don't be such a pussy," he said tilting his helmet to cover his eyes.

"How long have you wanted to drive that hot car?" While I was calculating the weeks, he answered his own question. "Since the first damn day."

"Yeah, I guess so."

"Besides," he said matter-of-factly, "next week you'll be spell man."

He surprised me with the news. "Why's that?"

"I'm goin' home to Memphis. My sister sent me a letter. My grandmother is failing, and she wants me to come down to say goodbye to her."

"I'm sorry to hear that," I said. Then I thought, *Your sister?* He never talked about his family, though I knew he must have one—everybody does. I mentioned my family from time to time, but I had never thought to ask him about his. We were work buddies, I guess, and that was about it.

"Me and my wife are taking the Greyhound later this evening."

"You never told me you had a wife." For six weeks, I'd worked with Theo and knew next to nothing about him.

"Well, you never asked. I have a young boy who is almost four also."

"Are you going to see your parents while you are there?" I thought now might be a good time to ask.

"I don't want to talk about them!" he said abruptly closing that door. "You up for the job?"

"You're not playing me now?"

"Sarge asked me to recommend a replacement, and I recommended you."

"Then he's okay with it?"

"Do you want the job or not? I need some fuckin' sleep."

"Get some rest and I'll catch you later." I snatched up my pocket radio and left the shed chuckling, knowing that in five minutes he'd be cursing me.

I traveled along the top of the ovens, slid down a couple of ladders, and was at the wharf in no time. I didn't mind pulling gates once I got the hang of it. My upper-body strength had increased and my chest and arm muscles firmed up. I was in the best shape I had ever been in. Normally, I could empty the wharf before the next load was dropped. There was method to this madness.

The admiral had dropped his fourth load when Bull

returned with his coffee, and I headed for the hot car. I'm sure the admiral had no notion I was about to spell him because he wasn't comfortable with handing his hot car over to me.

"Where's that peckerwood, Theo?"

"He's not feeling well. I'm here to spell you."

"Bullshit."

"Really! I'm filling in for him next week. Theo has family matters to attend to."

"You know what you're doing?"

"Shit yes!" I lied. "Any advice?" I said, not wanting to appear too cocky.

"Don't run out of fuckin' track."

"Thanks for the tip."

"One more thing, kid," he said making the sign of the cross. "Give me time to walk away, so I don't have to watch."

Just before he dropped out of sight, I ran the hot car up and down the track to get a feel for it. It worked like the old elevators in Hudson's department store downtown. I had marveled at them as a kid, but instead of going up and down, this went back and forth. I lined up the car with the door machine and waited for the glowing coke to fall into the car. It was spectacular in the darkness. With a slight jerk, I drove forward to distribute the load evenly in the car's bed, but I misjudged my speed. The burning coke tumbled off the cab's roof and slid onto the rail bed.

"Shit!" I said driving the car into the quenching

station. I looked behind at the glowing coke on the track, and then I was startled by the roar of screaming steam. After the deluge, I raced back up the track to where Bull was leaning on a gate, facing an empty wharf. I stopped the hot car and smiled; then I dumped the steaming coke and piled the whole load over five gates instead of easing it along the length of ten. The trick was to spread the coke out evenly, so the least amount of energy was used to lift the gate and load it onto the belt below.

The chief's eyes bugged out as he struggled to open an overloaded gate. "Are you crazy, kid? What the hell are you doing?" he shouted.

I tried to soften my embarrassment with humor. "It's called on-the-job training," I shouted back.

Bull Rider failed to see the humor. "If you can't handle the job, find someone who can." Bull was easy to be around unless you made his job harder than it had to be. Overloading a gate made it much harder for him to open; he had to be pushing seventy years old.

"I'll do better next time. I'm a quick learner."

"You sure as hell better be, goddamn it!"

I made another run that was only slightly better.

The admiral couldn't make himself stay away for his whole break. "Get your ass out of my hot car, you son of a bitch!"

"So you know my mom, huh?"

"Show some respect, asshole! She's the only mother you're ever gonna have. Now beat it, kid!"

His defense of my mother, a woman he didn't know, surprised me. There was more to him than I had given him credit for. "Thanks for the advice," I said walking away.

"And don't spell me no more. I'll shit in a bucket next time."

The admiral was tense and glad to see me vacate his hot car. It was time to wake Theo so he could finish the rest of his shift, and I could nap until sunrise.

8

Just Another Bum from the Neighborhood

B*uying that first car* is a coming-of-age ritual for any young American male, but especially so for a Detroiter. It is embedded in the culture and imbued in the gene pool. Young males huddling around and peering under the hood of some old wreck was a common sight in the days when a person could actually work on his own car. Almost everybody tinkered with his car because we grew up around tools and grease guns; it came honestly to most of us.

People in the Detroit area took pride in the nickname "the Motor City," and they took it to heart by supporting the local economy. "Buy American!" was the battle cry of the Big Three: Ford, General Motors, and Chrysler. But I wasn't answering the call. Muscle cars like Corvettes, Mustangs, and Chargers were the cars of choice for males of my generation, but I wanted something out of the ordinary that I could afford. That narrowed down the field considerably, so on my long weekend, I bought a new Volkswagen Beetle for under two thousand dollars and proudly drove it home.

"That's a foreign car," was my mother's first response. "You couldn't buy American?"

"It gets twenty-nine miles a gallon, Ma. With regular gas selling for thirty-five cents a gallon, I'll save lots of money when I commute to Ypsi." That was my ace in the hole.

"Why not stay in town and go to Henry Ford Community College?"

"I'll still need a car," I countered.

"And you had to get a yellow one. It looks like a lemon." She pinched her face up in a knot and walked into the house without saying another word. *That was easier than I thought it would be.*

Her reaction was not unexpected. Though it was disappointing, I didn't allow it to deter me from enjoying my new car. I sat behind the wheel and inhaled the new-car smell with intoxicating effect. The mixture of new lacquer and fresh vinyl interior was unmistakable. I wasn't going to let my mom's response spoil the romance between me and my ride. I was reading the owner's manual like it was great literature when my mother walked over to me with a book in her hands. It was a pictorial history of World War II. Using one of her thumbs as a bookmark, she opened to a photo of Adolf Hitler riding in a Volkswagen prototype in the late 1930s.

"Hitler was the mastermind behind that Nazi car," she sneered.

Ferdinand Porsche, who was riding beside Hitler in the photo, was the true intellect behind the "people's car." I wanted to tell her, "Ideas are easy; engineering is not," but I knew she wouldn't appreciate that argument, so why aggravate her more? She was already angry because my uncle Patrick had cosigned the loan for me, which she regarded as a betrayal and a personal affront. I had sidestepped her seal of approval and blessing in the decision-making process. For me, it was a bid for independence; for her, it was a loss of parental power and control, and she wouldn't forget it.

"That's the past. It was twenty-five years ago. Move on for goodness' sake."

But to her, the war was only yesterday. "Your uncle Joseph died fighting those Nazi bastards. Doesn't that mean anything to you?"

"Mom! That was four years before I was born. I never even knew the man."

"That man was your flesh and blood. Don't you have any family loyalty?"

"The army buried him. Maybe you should too."

"Is nothing sacred to you, smartass?"

This argument was going in a direction I didn't want, but I took the bait anyway, "I'll go to church and light a candle for him on Memorial Day."

"Listen, ingrate. I'm glad your father isn't here to see and hear this bullshit! He'd stick his foot up your ass so fast." As much as anything, she missed his parental muscle.

"If sticking his foot up my ass would bring him back to life, I'd bend over for him."

"Where did you get that mouth?"

"At home!" My remark only slowed her rant.

"Jake, are you crazy? This is Detroit! We've got family and friends in every plant in town. You couldn't buy American? What am I supposed to say to people?"

"Tell them I went nuts. They suspect that anyway."

My mom, as usual, had the final word on the subject. "I'll never ride in that Nazi car. Never!" she said walking back into the house.

Big surprise. She didn't want me to get any car in the first place. How was I supposed to commute to college without a son-of-a-bitchin' car? She had distracted me enough that I could only thumb through the rest of the owner's manual rather than read it like I wanted to do. The days of knee-jerk, robotic compliance to my mother's every whim or edict were over, and we both knew it.

I needed to show off my VW to someone who would appreciate it; I still had a couple of high school friends who hadn't gone off to college or the service yet. Jimmy McKinney was in no hurry to set the world on fire. Both of his parents worked, so Jimmy was on his own all day. His father was a line foreman for Garwood Industries in Wayne, where they made garbage trucks, and his mother was my English teacher at our local high school. She taught me to love the classics in tenth grade. When I got thrown out of the university, she was as upset and disappointed as my mother was. Mrs. McKinney thought I showed "promise." I actually read most of the books she assigned and could talk in her class about them.

On my days off, Jimmy and I played eight ball in his basement and listened to his vast collection of 45 rpm records of soul music and rhythm and blues. His mother loved the old torch singers like Lena Horne, Della Reese, and Diana Washington, so we never lacked for great music. Since high school graduation, Jimmy hung around the house most days, watching television and listening to music all day.

Without going back into the house to say goodbye to my mom, I started the motor on the Bug and wound out my gearbox going to Jimmy's house. I would let my mother stew in her own juices by herself for awhile. I felt bad being a disappointment to her all the time, but I only felt that way when I was at home. Jimmy lived only two short blocks from me, so I took the long way around to bond with my car for a few extra minutes. I wanted the new-car smell to last forever and breathed deeply to savor it. I could swear that I swooned a bit because the hydrocarbons in the paint were still curing, so I rolled down the window for some fresh air.

It was almost 11:00 AM when I pulled into the driveway and walked up to Jimmy's front door. I knocked several times and leaned on the doorbell until he dragged himself out of bed and answered it. As usual, his parents were working and he was still sleeping. *Nothing new there.* He pulled his fingers through his disheveled hair with one hand and scratched his crotch inside of his boxers with the other. Through unfocused eyes, he said dryly, "Yeah, man. What's up?"

"I came by to show you my new ride!" I beamed.

His eyes were still adjusting to the daylight. He squinted at my car in his driveway. "A Bug, cool."

He still wasn't totally awake, but his response was better than my mom's at least. "Throw on some clothes and we'll go for a cruise."

"Come on in and shoot some pool. I need to shower first."

It seems like I spent half my life in high school waiting for him. Sitting around on a rare day off of work wasn't a good use of my time, but I waited patiently for thirty minutes reading *Reader's Digest*. Finally, he lumbered out of his bedroom with his Army surplus combat boots and his green fatigue jacket in his hands. Sitting down in a recliner, he slowly began to put on his socks and lace up his high-top boots. That seemed to take another ten minutes.

"How about we make some breakfast first?"

"It's almost noon for Christ's sake, you lazy bastard. We'll get lunch at Virgil's Grille." This was our hangout when we cut classes in high school. They made the best from-scratch French fries and frothy malted milkshakes.

"We can't."

"Why not?"

"They went out of business a few months ago." Then he paused slightly. "Besides, I'm broke." Jimmy had never held a job and always complained about being broke. The guy was almost nineteen years old, and he was still waiting for his mom to give him his allowance for doing chores he should have been doing for free, especially since he contributed nothing to the household.

Get a job, buddy, I thought. During my last year of high school, I shook the grease out of French fries and beat air into shakes for McDonalds, and I had the zits to prove it.

"I'll treat you to lunch. I'm celebrating." It was almost an hour before we finally left his house, so I couldn't resist a dig. "Ever think about getting a job and some self-respect?"

"Now you sound like my mother."

"She's a smart lady. I could do worse."

"Jesus Christ, Jake! What's climbed up your ass?"

"A work ethic. You need to get a job, man."

"Why?"

Even in high school, Jimmy was aloof. He was a science geek who needed to work on his social skills. When we dissected a cat for biology class, he skinned the calico he was given, salt-cured the hide, and made a pencil bag out of it. That pretty much killed him as date material in high school. We, his loyal friends, couldn't buy him a date on prom night. Setting him up was impossible.

I had a tough time understanding Jimmy. Success or failure was all the same to him—he wasn't concerned with either. I wondered how far he would ride the logjam of lethargy. "Christ almighty. Don't you get bored hanging around the house all the time? Why not work at the mill with me? There is always a high turnover rate there."

"Get on a schedule? Be productive? Join the rat race?"

"Right! Why not?"

"Working with a bunch of coons and getting filthy dirty all the time isn't for me. Besides, all you do is work those crazy shifts. What do you do except work anymore? I almost never see you."

Jimmy's racial slur surprised and annoyed me because that wasn't something he commonly did, unlike almost everybody else we knew. He was also sounding like a neglected girlfriend, and that troubled me even more. "After a hard shift of working, I sit around donut shops and diners and shoot the shit with my 'coon' buddies."

"Now don't get all pissed off," he said getting into my car.

"At least these fuckers are working." I steered the conversation towards my car. "What do you think about my wheels?"

"It's smaller than the Rambler inside. The windshield is pretty close to my face."

I popped the clutch in first gear, and his head lunged towards the safety glass. The V-Dub stalled. "Sorry, I'm not used to the clutch." *Next time he says something cute about my car,* I thought, *I'll put his empty head through the windshield.*

"I like this handle above the glove box," he said holding on with both hands.

"There's one above the passenger door for taking hard turns," I said as I turned sharply left and jammed Jimmy against the passenger door.

"Slow down, for Christ's sake."

"I just wanted to show you how it handles."

"What! Like the fuckin' Wild Mouse at Edgewater Park?"

"Okay, okay. I was just playing with you."

We cruised through West Dearborn up Outer Drive to Michigan Avenue and east to Oakwood Boulevard until we got to Village Road, which curved between Greenfield Village on the left and the Ford Proving Grounds on the right. It was a fun, curvy stretch of road to wind out my gear box. Once we hit the Southfield Freeway, the fun and games were over. Competing with aggressive truck drivers and full-sized gas guzzlers at eighty miles an hour required my full attention just to stay out of their way.

"I don't get it! Why does a smart guy like you work in a dirt pit like Zug Island?"

"You're sitting in it, pedestrian."

"Touché!"

It is nice to win an argument every so often, I thought. "Truce?"

"Truce."

We decided to have lunch at Elias Brothers' Big Boy on Southfield Road in Allen Park. I pulled into a spot with curb service and ordered from an intercom menu. Fifteen minutes later, a waitress brought a tray filled with food and attached it to my driver's side window. It was Cheryl Cunningham from high school.

After a brief moment of startled recognition, she said, "Hey. How are you doing, Jake?"

She was one of my ex-girlfriend's best friends. How a person has more than one best friend is beyond me, but women seem to manage it. "Cheryl, I didn't expect to run into you here."

"Well, I'm working part-time to pay for my books at JC. What do you think of my uniform?" she said, turning around. "It's the latest fashion." Cheryl ended with a slight curtsy and saw Jimmy through my open car window smirking at her. Her pleasant face turned sour, like she had just belched up some stomach acid.

"Hey, what's a girl like you working in a nice place

like this?" Jimmy quipped. He didn't care for Cheryl—she'd refused to go with him to the homecoming dance in the eleventh grade.

"You know what I think of you, douche bag?" she said.

"Enlighten me, princess."

"Absolutely nothing."

"Be nice, butthole," I said, handing Jimmy his Big Boy burger and fries, hoping to shut him up.

I redirected my attention to Cheryl. I didn't care much for her in high school either, but she looked kinda foxy in her work uniform, which appealed to my newfound blue-collar persona. "It sure beats my work getup," I continued picking up the thread of our conversation, "a hard hat and a pair of steel-toed boots."

"Yeah, I heard you were taking a vacation from college."

"Thanks for putting it that way. Who'd you hear it from?" I knew the answer—Lynette, my old girlfriend.

"Is this sweet Beetle yours?"

"Sure is."

"I love the color. It's so ... European!"

"I really like it too."

"Where are you working, Jake?"

"A place called Zug Island. It's a part of Great Lakes Steel."

"Yeah, I know it. My uncle operates a crane there. Wow! That's heavy industry. How do you like it?"

"Gotta work someplace." I shrugged.

"Tell me about it. I need to get going, or I'll be looking for a job."

The check was about seven bucks, so I gave her a ten and called it even. I knew that would bug the shit out of Jimmy. "Keep the change."

"Thanks, I can use it. How about a ride sometime, handsome?" Cheryl had never cast an eye or an encouraging word my way before; of course, I was going with her girlfriend at the time, but that water was over the dam now. Maybe it was time to take the plunge.

"I'll call you when I get some spare time."

"Promise?"

"Sure," I smiled. "Good seeing you."

"You too," she said as she hurried to catch up with her next order.

I turned and looked at Jimmy. "Be careful not to mess up my new car," I said.

"Hell. You're sounding like my mother again," he complained with a mouthful of burger. "So, are you going to take Cheryl out?"

"Like you give a shit."

"You know what a stiff-assed snob she was in high school. She barely gave us the time of day."

"She barely gave you the time of day," I said between bites of onion rings. "Unlike us, she participated in school."

"She was a cheerleader, for Christ's sake!"

"As I remember it, you were fixated on her pompoms."

"Hey! I never laid a hand on her."

"That's not how I heard it."

"Over the sweater doesn't count, Casanova."

After a long sip on my Coke, I thought I'd yank his chain some more. "You're jealous?"

"Eat some shit, fuckwad."

"How nice! And while I'm feeding your sorry ass, too. Talk about biting the hand ..."

"Don't play coy with me. She really came on to you. She's not so high and mighty anymore now that she's wearing a waitress uniform," he sneered.

"At least she has a job."

"Low blow. We made a deal."

"Maybe she's just growing up. You should try it," I countered.

Jimmy's shiftless attitude annoyed me. "What are you going to do with the rest of your life? Watch the boob tube and masturbate all day?"

"No. But that doesn't sound bad."

"Then what is your master plan, Einstein?"

That's when Jimmy dropped his bomb. "Show up at Fort Wayne on Monday for my draft physical," he said.

His future plans had been made for him. After the unexpected news, his mood made more sense to me. I felt terrible for riding him all afternoon about being just another shiftless bum from the neighborhood.

"When did you get your notice?"

"Last week. 'Greetings, motherfucker...' it started. You know the rest."

"Maybe you'll luck out like me and get a 4-F deferment."

"I'm not that lucky. Anyway, why would I want flat feet?"

"They might keep you out of a rice paddy."

"I know one thing for sure, looking down the end of a rifle appeals to me more than looking down the end of a shovel or being a cog in a never-ending wheel making rust buckets. I hate this fucking godforsaken town."

Normally, I might have taken some offense at his remarks, but I knew the dilemma he faced. The same fate I faced several months before, the feeling of being trapped with no place to go. Jimmy had one thing figured out though. I never called Cheryl back. She was still friends with Lynette, and I needed a much larger turning circle than that.

9 The Shakedown Cruise

After a couple of days into the day shift, Theo returned from Memphis tired and saddened, so I hoped I could cheer him up after work when I proudly showed him my new car in the parking lot.

"Good work, Jake," he said nodding his head gently up and down. "It's small but stylish. What the hell is it?"

"It's a Volkswagen Beetle, made in Germany."

He opened the door and poked his head inside. "Emmm, I like that smell!" He didn't give a damn about the Nazis or the auto workers. Finally, somebody appreciated my car as much as I did.

"Man, I forgot about you getting a car. I thought sure you'd show up in a used Valiant or a Falcon."

"Come on, hop in!"

Theo scrunched all six feet of himself into the passenger seat, his knees tucked snuggly under the glove box. "Nice and cozy," he said smiling.

I took him for a short spin through the parking lot and fishtailed, doing a few figure eights on the gravel. I was sure I had worn the tread off my tires, but I was doing what most young male drivers do—burning off a little testosterone and a little rubber. I pulled up next to his car and slid to a stop. "What do you think?"

He laughed. "Goddamn, you drive like a maniac." He got out, stretched his lanky body, and checked for broken bones.

Alonzo Sanchez watched us from across the parking lot while putting his work gear into the trunk of his Cadillac. "What do you think of my wheels?" I asked him.

He turned towards my car and made the sign of the cross as a priest would bless the faithful; then he kissed the gold crucifix which always hung around his neck. "It kinda looks like a lemon, son. All yellow and all."

"Yeah, I heard that one before. It's fun to drive."

"It looks like a toy, that's for sure."

"It gets great gas mileage."

"How you gonna pick up some lovely young señorita in that, compadre?"

"That wasn't on my mind when I bought it."

"Silly boy," he sneered, shutting the trunk on his Cadillac. "Give me an El Dorado any day, amigo. It's a bedroom on wheels, numbnuts."

"Give Jake a break," Theo stepped in.

"I meant no disrespect. When you get to be middle-aged like me, you can't stand all that jostling around. I'm built for comfort, not economy." He smiled. "They call it a Bug, but it looks like a pregnant roller skate."

I wanted to say, "You Cuban old fart, screw you," but I didn't want to make an enemy of him, so I let him rib me.

Alonzo wasn't particularly liked by anyone on the island. The crew called him Pinto Bean, but not to his face. He was a shady character who transferred from the main plant in Ecorse for unspecified reasons, though the rumor mill said he had an affair with a manager's wife at the main plant, and Alonzo did nothing to deny or discourage the plant gossip. Nobody knew for sure, and that's how he kept it. All I knew for certain was that he sold marijuana and Dexedrine on the island. Alonzo spun up some ice and gravel at us as his big-assed car fishtailed away.

I now knew that this car was made for me. Hardly anybody liked it. About a week later or so, I was browsing through the United Steel Workers newspaper and saw a photo of a VW with the caption: "These Bug Us." The union didn't like foreign cars, true, but the rank-and-file steelworkers didn't give a damn for the most part. I had been parking in the company lot, but nothing ever happened to my car. After their shift, the workers just wanted to shower and get off the island as quickly as possible. Hell, they didn't build cars.

I was actually glad I didn't work at an automobile plant. The United Auto Workers had no sense of humor about foreign cars and were downright hostile about them. My mom was right. In Detroit, the Big Three ruled. Some of the brotherhood were known to throw a brick through the windshield or take a hammer to the sheet metal of a foreign car to drive their point home.

From time to time, the local television news programs would run special-interest segments showing autoworkers paying a dollar a whack to smash a Japanese car, usually a Toyota, with a ten-pound sledgehammer. Of course, the local news anchors played it off as a harmless fundraiser and a way for frustrated factory workers to let off some stream.

If Detroit's economy was bad or the UAW was on strike, look out! But I didn't care. This was America, and I could buy any goddamn car I wanted. Besides, there were so many German Americans in the Detroit area that I decided to take my chances, and I never had a problem.

Another week passed and Theo's mood hadn't improved. He had taken the word of his grandmother's death pretty hard. His Grandma Lilly had raised him from childhood. When he had visited and seen her at the hospital in the bed she would die in, she was barely conscious and didn't have the strength to recognize him.

One day, we were eating lunch from the end of the battery overlooking the thawing river.

"Are you feelin' okay?" I asked him.

"Yeah, I just got the blues, that's all," he said, like depression was the most natural thing in the world.

"At least the weather is getting better. Springtime feels great."

"What?"

I knew what was bothering him. "That's tough that your grandmother didn't recognize you," I told him.

"As close as you are to me, and she didn't know I was there."

"You knew you were there. I'm sure your sister was grateful you went back. There was nothing else you could do. You did the right thing, bro'." That was the first time I had called him that. I thought now might be a good time to ask him about his parents. Theo had never so much as mentioned them to me. "It must've been good to see your folks while you were there."

He got real quiet before he answered, "Not much family left."

"What about your sister?"

"Oh, yeah," Theo said lost in thought. "We stayed with Darlene and her three kids. She was half crazy with sadness and worry that she worked herself into a nervous condition. Reminded me why I moved away."

It was my turn to be quiet now.

"I never knew my father," he continued without prompting. "I was told he died in Korea. We have one bent-up photograph of him in his dress uniform standing in front of a palm tree, taken in Hawaii before he shipped out."

I was still getting over the death of my own father, so I fell into the same somber mood. Misery loves company. "I think about my father every day, and I wonder what he'd think about me working here." Suddenly, I flashed on what Scotty, the supervisor, told me my first day—"Make your goddamned money and get the hell out of here."

We both sat gazing blankly across the river where we could see the trees starting to green up in the distance. "What about your mother? Was she there to help your grandmother at the end?"

"My mother, god rest her soul, couldn't afford to raise me and my sister alone, so she ran off to Memphis and left us in the country with my grandmother when I was five and my sister was three. She worked at some clubs and sent money back when she could. But she never wrote a letter."

"That's odd. Why didn't she write?"

"Never learned how, I guess."

That surprised me. "What kind of clubs did she work at?"

"She was a 'hostess' working the downtown clubs. That's what we call bars in the South."

"A hostess?"

"Christ Almighty! Don't you know anything?" After a pause, he continued. "She was a working girl, a whore. I barely can remember her. A couple of farm boys found her body one Sunday morning while they were giggin' for fish. They found her floating facedown, half-naked in an irrigation ditch, next to some cotton patch in Arkansas."

My only response was an inadequate: "That's tragic." It was all I could think to say.

"I never told anybody that before," he said lighting a cigarette. He peered into the unfocused distance. "They found her strangled with her bra and wearing part of her torn dress. The current in the irrigation ditch had carried her body down the channel until the dress got hung up on some underbrush. These farm boys were spear fishing their way upstream when they found her all bloated and smelly. Fish and small animals had been feeding on her body for a couple of days."

"For goodness sake! And you never told your wife that story?" I continued.

"My wife?" he said vacantly.

"Yeah, that lady you're married to."

"I told her my mother had died when I was a kid but never went into the facts. She never asked. Doretha gets depressed easy enough on her own."

Theo allowed me to cross a threshold when he started telling me about his family. A bond was forming. "I'd like to meet your family sometime."

"Too late!" He took a deep drag on his Kool before letting the smoke out slowly. "She and my son stayed down there with her relatives."

"Why?"

"She's lonely, and I'm gone working as much as I can. Besides, it's too cold for her here; she hates it up in the North. Her only friends are some church ladies who are always hovering around. Her kin are all back in Tennessee. The night before I returned to Detroit, she told me she wasn't coming back with me. I tried to change her mind, and she cried in my arms, but I couldn't make her coming back with me."

Theo was laid-back by nature, but this real-world drama would depress anyone. I was surprised he revealed as much as he had. It was clear he needed someone to talk with, so I listened and he told me an earful.

"Doretha was fifteen and I was sixteen when I put her in the family way the first time. She wanted to keep the baby, so I married her when she turned sixteen. We were doing all right until she lost the baby."

"Lost the baby," I said, more as a response than a question.

"Then she got the miseries and went a little numb on the inside. You know?" he said looking toward me, then away again.

"I can imagine," I lied. What did I know of a woman's grief over the loss of a child?

"We tried again and again until we had a son

two years later. He was born a premie. Little Otis survived after a struggle bein' born in the emergency room at County Hospital. Things were tough for us in Tennessee, work was scarce, and wages were low. When I heard about jobs up North, we both thought a change of scenery would help, so I came to Detroit first to get settled, and after a few months, I put aside enough money to send for my family. Doretha hated the weather and missed her kin from the start. She had been thinking about separating from me and returning home for a long time. Visiting my ailing grandmother provided her the opportunity to move back in with her folks."

"Wow. Anything good ever happen to you, man?"

"Not much, I guess," he said, finishing his cigarette and flicking it in the air. He stared looking south down the river.

"I guess you do have a bad case of the blues."

"Amen to that."

"What do you say we go on that power cruise after work tonight?" I asked trying to get his mind off his troubles.

"Yeah. Why not?" he said with a mild hint of enthusiasm.

"First, I need to know where to pick you up."

"It's easy," he said scribbling his address on a paper napkin and offering it to me. "I'm renting a room not far from here."

"Where are you going tonight, dear?" I heard my mother ask through the locked bathroom door while I was blow-drying my hair after my first trip to the barber in weeks. I turned off the hair dryer, ran the comb through my hair, made a few gentle hand adjustments, and held it all in place with a spritz of hair spray over the entire mess. "Out, Mom!"

"Out? Where out? Damn it, Jake! 'Out' is what I should have said to you three months ago when you got kicked out of school."

I let that remark pass and switched off the light, unlocked the door, and came out of the bathroom smelling like Canoe and Aquanet. My mother gave me the once-over; even my leather shoes were polished and my fingernails were trimmed and cleaned, as well as I could get them, considering the job I had. "Yeah, Mom! I'm going out tonight," I said like I didn't hear her before.

"Do you have a date, honey?"

"Not really."

"So, what are you doing tonight?"

I enjoyed the mild bantering with her. This brief conversation was the most normal moment my mother and I'd had together since I returned home.

"Well, I didn't want to say anything, but ..."

"Yes!" she yipped. "You and Lynette are back together. I knew it would happen. How wonderful!" It was apparent that my mother had fonder memories of her than I did.

"Not quite, Mom."

"Then who?" She looked vaguely disoriented.

Now I had to scramble fast for a story. I wasn't ready to tell her that I was going to cruise the town with Theo; then she would give me the third degree about it. She was already fearful for my safety and desperate not to lose the last survivor of our small family. *Better not to upset her.*

"Remember I told you I ran into Cheryl a few weeks ago?"

"The waitress at Big Boy's?"

"Yes, she's the one."

Looking like she was finding it hard to comprehend, she said, "That friend of Lynette's? That tramp who broke Jimmy's heart?"

I was enjoying this. "Yeah, that's her."

"Well, I know her mother—a divorcée. She's a barmaid and God knows what else. I learn a whole lot working at the florist shop. That woman gets more flowers sent to her from different men than Evergreen Cemetery." She looked at the ceiling and her head shuddered like she was a palsy victim. With palms raised to the ceiling she warned, "Bad blood begets bad blood. That's all I'm saying."

"Good, because that's all I'm going to listen to." The conversation suddenly wasn't any fun anymore.

"What do you know about this girl?"

"We went to high school together, and she's a

student at Henry Ford Community College. She waitresses to pay for her textbooks."

"What's your attraction to her?"

"She's blond and an ex-cheerleader," I said, kissing my mother on the cheek. I grabbed my windbreaker and headed for the side door.

"What time will you be home?"

"Don't wait up for me."

"Oh, Lord."

Theo Semple roomed just outside the Detroit city limits in the city of River Rouge. At about eight that evening, I found the Victorian house where he was renting and knocked on the front door. Nobody answered. I never knew of anyone outside of a Hollywood movie who lived in a boarding house. It seemed like something from a bygone age. I opened the huge wooden door and could swear I was entering the *Psycho* house. I cautiously walked up a flight of stairs and found his room, number five, and knocked.

Once again, no one answered. I was about to knock a little harder when a creaking door at the end of the hallway surprised me. Theo walked out of the community bathroom, all duded up with his hair slicked back. He had on narrow black pants, a purple satin shirt, and shiny dress shoes. He looked like one of the Temptations. I couldn't believe the transformation.

"Getting ready?" I prompted him.

He instantly picked up the cue, "Getting ready and here I come… Getting ready and here I come," he sang strolling down the hall. His mood had improved greatly from earlier in the day. He unlocked his door, and we entered. His room had a mattress sitting on a simple metal frame, a wooden chair, a chest of drawers with an AM table radio on top, and a picture of a blue-eyed Jesus on the wall, pointing to his sacred heart. He slipped on a black leather jacket and took a hat he called a stingy brim from a coat rack in the corner. He placed it strategically on his head. "Ready!"

"Let's go," I said. Theo and I couldn't have looked any different. I was wearing khaki pants, a madras print buttoned-down shirt, and a navy blue windbreaker, all from Sears. We were an odd-looking pair to be sure. *Mutt and Jeff*. I wondered where we might go so we wouldn't attract any unwelcome attention. "Where to?"

"First, the liquor store. Then, who cares?"

We got in my car and headed south on West Jefferson until we found a party store. "I want some sloe gin. What do you want?"

I wasn't drinking since I had moved back home but said a six-pack would do me.

"Too many bottles. We're out on the town. How about some Mohawk lime vodka?

"Sure. I'll try anything once."

He bought the pints and returned to the car.

"Where to?" I asked.

He shrugged his shoulders. After almost two years, he didn't know the area very well and didn't have any friends as far as I knew. Now that he was separated from his wife, he was even more isolated.

I drove to Ecorse Park at the end of Southfield Road. There was a walkway along the shoreline of the river with benches every so often used by people fishing, lovers with no place else to go, or losers like us who were just hanging out drinking. We sat in the car and drank for awhile. The lime vodka was wretched until it went to work on my central nervous system; after my gag reflex relaxed, it didn't seem so bad. Less than fifteen minutes later, we got bored and drove towards the city.

I knew of plenty of places to hang out in the suburbs, but I didn't want to cross any color lines. Racism was alive and widespread in the area. *It isn't that I don't want to be seen with him,* I said unconvincingly to myself. I just knew better and wanted to avoid the hassle. No controversy tonight! The truth was I didn't have the courage to be seen with him. I racked my mind for someplace safe to go.

"Why don't we head up to Belle Isle?" I suggested.

"Sounds good to me."

Belle Isle was an island park considered neutral territory, where blacks and whites could mingle with relative freedom. It seemed comfortable enough because I didn't think I'd run into anyone I knew there. I turned right on West Jefferson and headed north. "You feeling any better, Theo?"

"Than what?"

"Than the boil on my butt, for Christ's sake."

He took a tug on his sloe gin. "Much better now that we have a couple of days off." Theo sat there glowing with a contented smile on his face.

"You sure look and sound better than you did this morning."

He nodded his head agreeably.

"What are you smiling about?"

"This is the first time I've ever gone cruising with a white guy," he confessed.

"You're kidding," I remarked as if this were routine and natural for me.

"How about you?"

"Naw! I've hung out with lots of white guys."

We laughed and tugged on our pints some more.

"You crazy bastard," Theo said. "You know what I mean."

"Yeah, I do. You're the first black guy I've hung out with. The only black people I've been around were at my college and they didn't mingle much."

"Why is that?"

So I gave him my take on it. "The black and white students at my university didn't mix much, except on the sports field. Most students seemed to gravitate into their own racially isolated fraternities and sororities."

"That doesn't surprise me."

"It does me. Different environment, same old shit."

"What fraternity were you in?"

"None," I said with pride. "I was a GDI."

Theo made a face that looked like he was sucking on a lemon. "What the hell is a GDI?"

"A goddamned independent!"

"Unpopular?" he said, looking at me.

"You got it!"

"Really?"

"No, asshole. I got enough of that schoolboy shit in high school."

"Workin' with us must be a real shock for you."

"With who?" I played dumb.

"With black folks, fool."

"Not anymore. Like everyone else on the island, I'm there to make money. Working with black people isn't a problem for me. Hell, after about half an hour, I'm covered head to heel with coal dust like everyone else. It's a great leveler and very democratic."

"I'm glad to hear it. You know a difference between the North and the South I figured out?"

"Don't tell me! The South got the hell beat out of it in the Civil War."

"They call it the War Between the States in the South." Theo finished his pint while I was still nursing mine. Then he surprised me with this insight. "In the North, white people don't particularly mind working with black people, but whites don't want to live in the same neighborhood with blacks. In the South, it's different. We don't mind living in the same town, but Southern whites don't want to work alongside us."

That thought never crossed my mind. "Why do you think that is?" I asked.

"It's from years of being masters and slaves. Old habits die hard, Jake."

Before I could agree with him, I noticed flashing red lights in my rearview mirror and pulled over. "Oh, shit! The cops. Do something with those liquor bottles!"

"What liquor?" he said finishing my lime vodka before the police shined their spotlight into my back window. He shoved the empty pints under the seat, and I chewed on a stick of Juicy Fruit gum.

"Want some?"

"Hell no!" Theo lit up a cigarette. I didn't like him smoking in my car, but now wasn't the time to mention it to him.

We were almost up to East Grand Boulevard, the entrance to Belle Isle, when we were pulled over. I rolled down my window and looked into my rearview mirror. Both policemen had their hands on their service revolvers as they approached my VW.

"Yes, officer. What can I do for you?" I was taught to be polite to policemen.

"Get out of the car please," the lead cop said.

"Sure. What's wrong?"

"Out of the car, please."

"You too!" the backup cop commanded Theo.

"What for?" he protested blowing smoke rings out the passenger side window.

"I don't need a reason. Get your black ass out of the car!"

"I'd rather not."

I wondered why Theo was being stubborn. This was the last thing we needed. The cop pulled out his nightstick. I looked into the car with bulging eyes and motioned for him to please get out. He did, but not quickly enough to suit the policeman.

"Over to the sidewalk, away from the vehicle," the cop said pushing him to the curb. "Don't you look pretty tonight?" he taunted.

"Show me your driver's license," the lead cop ordered me.

I reached for my wallet, opened it, and showed him the license.

"Remove it from the wallet."

"Sure." I fumbled with it. "Here you go."

"Go stand over there with your ... buddy."

He returned to the patrol car and called in my plate number and driver's license number over his radio. I heard him use the expression "a snowball and a chunk of coal." The car wasn't stolen, and I didn't have any outstanding warrants or unpaid traffic tickets, so he couldn't hold us. He seemed disappointed but not surprised. Meanwhile, the other cop kept a cold eye on us standing on the sidewalk. "We're going to search your car!" First, he reached under the seats and found the pints. "What are these?"

"Empties, you fool," Theo antagonized back. I wished he would have kept his mouth shut.

"You're only eighteen, so tell your friend to curb his mouth before I take you both in." The cop reached in again, unlatched the front seats, and tossed them in the street; then, he lifted out the rear seat and did likewise. The only two things left in the car were a bag of White Castle hamburgers we were going to eat when we got to Belle Isle and my storage battery. "What's this?" the younger cop said carefully handling the closed bag like it was state's evidence. "Hey, Carl?"

The lead cop popped my front trunk and threw my spare tire and jack in the street amid the scattered litter surrounding my car. He didn't find anything except an empty cooler which landed with a hollow thump when it hit the pavement. "What, Art?" he said standing upright.

"They've been to Whities."

"Are you sure? There could be anything inside that bag."

The sliders were still warm and giving off their signature aroma as we saw them tumble to the street. I'd rather they had eaten them.

"Find anything?" said the straight man.

"Nope!" said the comic.

This scene was straight out of vaudeville. The next thing I expected was a street-theater version of "Here

Come Da Judge." There was only one explanation. This wasn't happening. It was all too absurd. What next?

The lead cop fell out of character long enough to get our attention.

"All right now! What are you guys up to tonight?"

"I'm taking my friend for a ride in my new car."

"Sure you are."

"Really! That's about it," I said as contritely as possible while Theo glared at them.

"White people don't hang out with colored people unless there's something going down. What's going down, tough guy?"

I knew he wouldn't be satisfied with "Nothing," so I tried the truth. "We were going down to Belle Isle to eat those burgers when you pulled us over."

"You expect me to believe that?"

"Why not? It's the truth."

"What kind of a fool do you take me for?"

Before Theo could make a knee-jerk remark, I answered, "I don't take you for any kind of fool, officer."

The cops were bored with us. "I don't want to see either of you guys on our beat again. Have a nice day!" he said, and they backed away to their patrol car.

As they pulled off, Theo fumed. "Goddamned pigs. I hate them."

"I guess we got off easy, huh?" I was trying to downplay the whole thing.

"Easy, my ass! They were just fuckin' with us. Look in the street for Christ's sake."

True. Half of what I owned in this world was lying there, but I still felt lucky they didn't arrest us.

"It could be worse; I'm a minor. They could've taken us both in."

"They didn't give a good goddamn about those pints!" he said. "They didn't like the idea of a white guy chauffeuring a nigger around."

"It doesn't pay to give the police shit, Theo."

"That's what they fuckin' count on!"

"They have the power."

"That's what they think."

I hadn't seen passion or anger in Theo before. I began to understand why African Americans have a deep-rooted distrust of the police and authority figures. I learned that it takes more than a badge or a uniform to command respect. My naïveté clashed with raw reality that evening. Theo and I put my car back together, picked up what we could of dinner, and went on our way hoping to avoid any more crime fighters before we reached Belle Isle.

10

Stations of the Cross

O*nce we hung a* right onto MacArthur Bridge, we entered Belle Isle and found the park almost deserted. We drove into a parking space near a bench on the west end, facing the Detroit skyline, and watched the iron-ore boats and freighters lumber upstream, battling the strong river current. Theo dragged on his cigarette without his usual sense of abandon, pushing the smoke out of his lungs and nose with irritation.

"Hell, that's all I need," I laughed, trying to lighten the mood. "Getting busted for underage drinking after getting kicked out of college for the same damn thing. That's rich!"

He nodded like he was listening, but his mind was elsewhere. I could tell by the way he picked the bit of tobacco from the tip of his tongue and flicked it into the darkness.

"My mom would have a field day with this. She'd be convinced that I'm a teenage alky and plant me in a rehab program somewhere." Still, he was unresponsive. "You're lucky the cops didn't arrest you for buying alcohol for a minor. They could have caused us a lot more trouble if they wanted to."

"Frick and Frack were just fuckin' with us."

"Well, thank heaven they didn't run us in."

"Heaven had nothin' to do with it. The lazy bastards didn't wanna do the paperwork. That's all."

"I'm just glad it's over."

"This shit happens to black folks every day."

I had never given police harassment much thought until I was the victim of it. As far as I knew, the police were there to serve and protect, not to harass people. Detroit may have been less than ten miles from my sheltered neighborhood in Dearborn, but it may as well have been in a different country. This wasn't the America I thought I knew.

"I need to get back to church. I've been feeling mighty empty lately."

"I didn't know you were a churchgoer."

"I go when I have a Sunday off. You know how seldom that is. Doretha was the one. She went twice a week and sang in the choir. Goin' to services was the main thing she did up here."

"You miss her a lot, don't you?"

"Sometimes, yes; sometimes, no."

I didn't want to delve any deeper into his marital

life. The April wind gusted off the river and sent up a sudden chill. We hadn't done much that evening, but an hour and a half was too soon to take him back to his place. I wasn't prepared for another a salt-and-pepper cruise downtown tonight, but I had an idea. "Do you like playing pool?"

"For money?"

"No, hustler! For recreation, for the fun of it."

He scrunched up his eyebrows. The idea seemed foreign to him, but it beat sitting on a breezy park bench. "Yeah, why not? I like shootin' stick."

"Well, let me warn you. I learned pool from my dad in our basement when I was growing up, and I'm pretty damned good," I said.

"I'll be careful," he taunted. "If you're so good, how about five dollars a game?"

"You're on!" I said. "There's a great pool parlor in Metro Airport that's open till midnight. What do you say?"

"What's wrong with a downtown pool hall?"

"They're dingy and smell like cigars," I said like I knew what I was talking about. My only experience with them was seeing the great Paul Newman movie *The Hustler*. "I promised you a power cruise. It's in Romulus, only twenty minutes outside of town in farm country."

Theo had never been to Detroit Metropolitan Airport, so we got back into the car and headed for the Edsel Ford freeway. While we were driving, he surprised me by asking if I would go to Sunday services with him.

"What?" I was hoping I hadn't heard him correctly. No such luck!

"You got something better to do Sunday?"

"Jeez ... church really isn't my thing, man." I squirmed and grimaced.

"Why not? We both have the day off."

I had been an atheist for a long time, but I didn't want to tell him that. He expressed a genuine interest in taking me to his church, so I didn't want to refuse him outright.

"I'm not a religious person, Theo." I hoped that he'd just drop it.

"You believe in God, though."

"I'm agnostic," I told him.

"What kind of religion is that?"

"It's a sect of the Catholic church."

"Oh," he responded, as if the word "Catholic" explained everything.

"What religion are you?" I asked.

"Southern Baptist."

"Like my grandmother," I said feigning interest.

"So? What about it? You come to my church and I'll go to yours."

I was afraid that was coming. "We'll see," I said noncommittally.

I hadn't believed in God since I was eight or nine years old. I wasn't allowed to make my First Communion because I skipped catechism so much I wasn't prepared. My mother had already addressed and stamped the announcements to family and friends when the Mother Superior, Sister Everest, phoned with the bad news.

"That's correct. He hasn't been to catechism for the last two months, and he won't be making his First Communion in May." I was certain Sister Everest took great delight in making an example of a public school catechism student, a lesson not lost on my Catholic school friends. When word spread through the parish, their moms wouldn't let them play with me anymore. That was all right, though. The neighborhood was full of other heathens and public school kids who were more my style anyway. "By the way," Sister Everest continued. "Is Jake short for the biblical name, Jacob?"

"I guess it is," my mother said as I noticed the wires begin to cross and short circuit behind her eyes.

"For parish records, we don't like to use nicknames."

"The name Jake is on my son's birth certificate and on his baptismal certificate."

"Jacob is more reverential. Don't you agree? So you may want to—"

My mother cut her off in mid-sentence, "We like

the boy's name the way it is, thank you! We'll use Jacob for his confirmation name."

"As you wish. May I suggest you enroll your son in Our Lady rather than public school? A spiritual rather than a secular education might do him some good."

My mother didn't take advice well, especially when she was angry. It was all she could do to keep from exploding. "I'll discuss it with my husband when he comes home from work. Thank you!" she said. I knew lightning would strike soon with terrible vengeance. I could hear the thunder approaching in the guise of my mother's churning stomach acids.

"Where have you been going on Mondays after school? And don't lie to me!"

I was dumbstruck. I needed to think on my feet.

Neither of my parents went to church regularly, but I was expected to go faithfully every Sunday with my younger brother Evan and attend catechism on Mondays after school as well. It was my first lesson in religious hypocrisy. I wasn't sorry for skipping catechism, but I was afraid of getting caught. I felt the devil that night in the form of strap leather and profanity. When the punishment ended, I was cured of my love of God and my fear of Satan.

Going to Theo's church might be a possibility, but going to mine was definitely out of the question. I hadn't gone to mass since I was in junior high school, when I pointed out to my mother that she and my father went to mass only on Christmas and Easter. She slapped my face for that bit of impertinence. Out of nowhere I said to her, "If it makes you feel more like a man, hit me again." After that, she never hit me or insisted that I attend weekly services, so it was worth it. It had been so long since I had gone to mass that I felt like I didn't even have a church to take him to anyway.

"What the hell! I'll go."

Theo seemed pleased. "Then we'll check your church out," he added.

"That part is problematic."

"What?"

"I haven't seen the inside of a church in years," I confessed. "Well, not since my father's funeral."

"I thought you told me you were Catholic? Take me to your Catholic church."

"Well … I was excommunicated." That excuse didn't play well with him.

"What's the problem? You ashamed to be seen in the House of God with me?"

That was an argument I could not win. After what we had gone through with the police, I didn't want to refuse his request, so I decided to tough it out. "I'll work through it," I told him as we turned into the airport parking lot. The rest of the evening, he gave me a lesson in eight ball and humility. I only had twenty dollars on me, so it didn't take that long.

The next Sunday we didn't work, Theo and I showed up for church services just before they began at 10:00 AM. Theo was dressed in his Sunday best, a full suit and tie but with no hat; I was wearing a brown corduroy sports coat I had just bought at Robert Hall's Men's Store. I didn't wear a tie but wore a v-neck vest with a white shirt underneath and thought it would do.

The Southern Baptist Tabernacle turned out to be a two-story, red-brick, 1920s-era storefront. I felt self-conscious as we entered the church, but after the congregation's initial reaction to us, the churchgoers smiled and seemed friendly enough, so I relaxed. Most of the people there were black, but there were some people of mixed race and several white women with black men also. I was the only single white male in the group that I could see. *Turnabout is fair play, I guess.*

At the front of the room, twelve choir members dressed in royal blue robes with silver shawls hanging from their necks sat in wooden folding chairs on a raised stage. The minister, dressed in a black robe with a golden shawl, held a large worn Bible in his right hand. He stood by, ready to battle Satan and his army of sinners. He seemed a dignified, slightly built man with penetrating eyes magnified by thick-lensed, plastic rimmed glasses that seemed large for his small face.

Reverend Jones began the services with a general greeting to the congregation and led them in a prayer; then he motioned to the choir to be seated. The choir sang two gospel songs to warm up the congregation. Hands started clapping and bodies began to move to the rhythm of the gospel spirituals. I must have been the only one who didn't know the songs because everybody else was singing. From the back of the room where we were sitting, it was difficult to distinguish the voices of the choir from the faithful because everyone sang with infectious passion and abandon. When they finished, Reverend Jones walked up to a simple podium, and everyone else sat down.

He opened his Bible to Genesis 19: The Destruction of Sodom and Gomorrah and the Story of Lot. He used the Bible more as a hand prop than a reference book, reciting scripture loosely and delivering commentary freely. "Evil must be destroyed, but 'Vengeance is mine,' saith the Lord."

The church members affirmed the preacher's message. "Amen" and "That's Right!" reverberated throughout the room.

"Lot obeyed the ancient laws of hospitality and protected his guests, angels sent by God, from an angry mob. The man put out a helping hand when he could have turned his guests away. He didn't do the easy thing; he did the right thing. Glory be!"

The call-and-response took on a life of its own.

"Yes, he did!"

"That's right!"

"Amen."

"Hallelujah."

"Jesus be praised."

"Glory be to God."

"Lot even offered his two daughters to the mob. Then God spoke to Lot, 'Take your family and flee for your lives,' said the Lord, 'but whatever you do, don't look back!' God commanded."

"That's right!"

"Amen."

"And God rained down fire and brimstone upon the wickedness of Sodom and Gomorrah."

"Praise Jesus!"

"You know the story ... Lot's wife, weak creature that she was, looked back and was turned into a pillar of salt. Give me an Amen!"

The response went around the room. The spiritual atmosphere was contagious, and I found myself being drawn into the service. Before he was finished, the reverend preached about perseverance in the face of adversity, unshakable belief in the Lord, unquestioning acceptance of what you cannot change, and obedience to God's will. Every person in that room was wet with perspiration and many wiped tears from their eyes. When he was finished, a lone piano pounded out a heavy rhythm and the choir stood up and blasted out another gospel song, "A Closer Walk with Thee," which spilled sweet harmony throughout the room and into the street.

After the service, everyone went down to the social hall in the basement, where the church ladies had prepared a potluck dinner. I couldn't keep my mouth from watering. The familiar smells wafted up from the basement midway through the service, and it was driving me crazy. They served fried and barbecued chicken, potato salad and Jell-O molds, spare ribs and baked beans, lemonade and coffee, hush puppies and grits, coleslaw and greens. And something I hadn't tasted since I had visited my grandmother in Tennessee as a kid—sweet potato pie.

Religion aside, I began to understand why Theo needed to go to church. He was disconnected and isolated, starved for community. He craved a sense of belonging that he couldn't get anywhere else, not to mention the weekly church buffet, which was the best meal I had had since senior prom night at Carl's Chop House.

The reverend mingled with his flock while everyone chatted, ate, and enjoyed each other's company. Eventually, he made his way over to us.

"It's good to see you again, son," he said shaking Theo's hand. "We've missed you and your wife."

I was amused that the reverend called Theo "son." That was my nickname.

"Thank you kindly, Reverend Jones."

"I've heard about your problems from some of the church ladies. We miss hearing Doretha's voice in our choir, but we know she missed her kin. Family is everything, son. It's the glue that binds the community together and keeps the mind and body whole."

"Yes, Reverend," Theo nodded. "She thought Otis is better off being raised with her folks than being here with me."

"Don't be bitter. Give her some time. God will sort it out for the best."

"A boy needs a father, Reverend."

"Amen to that. You know you're always welcome here, son."

"I appreciate that, Reverend." I could tell Theo felt edgy when he handed the preacher off to me. "I'd like you to meet my friend, Jake Malone from Melvindale."

The minister's ill-fitting glasses rode halfway down his nose. He lowered his chin and looked above his frames to see me better. "Thank you for coming," he said with a double-handed handshake. "We're always happy to see a new face in the congregation."

"I enjoyed the service, Reverend," I said looking him squarely in the face. His eyes were smaller and more penetrating when they weren't magnified behind his thick glasses. Any more than a quick glance and I feared he would read me like a matchbook cover. I wasn't sure whether I was confusing insight with severe myopia, but I wasn't taking any chances.

"We enjoyed having you too, son. Can we expect to see you again?"

"Most likely," I said to be polite. "You service was a revelation to me."

"Thank you, kindly. Enjoy some of Sister Kate's pecan pie while it's still warm." He leaned towards us and softly said, "It gets rock hard if it sits too long."

"Thanks for your hospitality, Reverend," Theo said as we worked our way over to the buffet table. We passed on the pecan pie, but the sweet potato pie looked and smelled delicious, so we each snagged some right off. Theo grabbed some cookies, Jell-O, spareribs, a couple of hush puppies, and a cup of coffee, while I snagged some fried chicken, potato salad, a glop of grits, and some lemonade. Good old homestyle Southern cooking.

"What do you think?" he asked as we sat down on some folding chairs along the back wall.

"The food smells heavenly; I can't wait to taste it."

"Forget the soul food for a minute. What about the church service?"

I wasn't sure what to say. I felt like I had seen a 3D movie, except with better picture and sound. I enjoyed the experience but didn't want to encourage him and make churchgoing a habit, so I simply said, "It was different." I knew only half of the bargain had been struck.

"Well, it made me feel better," he said. "On our next free Sunday, we'll visit your church."

I began to feel the church food genuflect in my stomach.

"Right?" he said.

"Sure," I said without enthusiasm. "Stranger things have happened."

It was early May before we had another Sunday off. I had been dreading this moment for the better part of a month, but a bargain is a bargain, so I planned to take Theo to eight o'clock Low Mass. If we waited until ten o'clock for High Mass, the church would be packed, and the service would be longer. That would only prolong my misery. During Low Mass, the priest speaks the parts of the Mass that are sung during High Mass and he omits the incense and holy water ritual at the beginning. Low Mass had no choir either, so I could cut another ten minutes from the charade.

It was a beautiful spring morning when I pulled into the parking lot of Our Lady of Perpetual Misery in Dearborn. I found a space close to the exit, so we could make a clean getaway after mass. My stress increased as we walked past two ushers and entered the church through ornately carved oak doors with heavy, weather-beaten brass hardware. A black man rarely, if ever, crossed the threshold of this church, and the ushers didn't know how to react or what to do. Theo wore his same Sunday suit like he did the last time we went to church, but this time with an open-collared shirt. I had on a white dress shirt again, but with a tie this time. We both looked presentable enough.

"Follow my lead," I whispered to Theo.

Automatically, I dipped my fingertips into the holy water font by the door and made the sign of the cross. I had told myself I wasn't going to bless myself when I entered the church, but my early Catholic conditioning kicked in at the last second. *Curious how that works sometimes!* Theo used his left hand and made the sign of the cross backwards, but we had cleared the second hurdle which relieved me somewhat.

The bright morning sun shining through the stained-glass rose window cast dappled colors on the pews. We chose a seat near the rear of the church. This apparently was Theo's first time in a Catholic church, and he looked around in awe. "Your church is like a palace," he said. The stained glass, statuary, paintings, candles, flowers, and the odor of stale frankincense had worked their ancient magic on him.

I looked around and was glad I didn't recognize anybody. I counted only about forty people, so rather than blend in, we stood out.

"I'm the only brother here," Theo whispered.

"No shit, Sherlock."

Just then, a petite, elderly grandmother with a dowager's hump slowly made her way up the aisle. She wore a long, black lace shawl to cover her head, and she carefully held the arm of a beautiful young woman with auburn hair neatly arranged beneath her spring bonnet. She must have been the old woman's granddaughter. The young woman eased her grandmother gently into a pew several rows ahead of us and noticed we were watching them as she sat down. She smiled. On some mad impulse, I winked at her, and to my surprise, she winked back.

Theo took notice and whispered, "I told you this church thing would work out for you."

"Right. Maybe I should drag her into the confessional and have sex with her; then I could ask for forgiveness at the same time. What do you think?"

"What's a confessional?"

I waved off the question. The mere thought of her and me together made my cheeks flush. My overactive fantasy life had a nasty habit of outrunning my real life. Why not add sacrilege to my other sins?

Ding ... ding ... ding. The striking of the altar bells broke the silence. The mass began with the litany read from St. Joseph's Daily Missal, with the programmed responses and the standing and kneeling of the parishioners, punctuated by the ringing of altar bells and the trinity of light-fisted beats upon the heart. The ritualism of the mass was lost upon Theo, though he looked quite interested in the medieval theater of it. The priest's vestments, especially the chasuble, the outer robe, caught his eye. The huge cross in white trimmed in gold and set against a green background must have made Theo think the priest was a crusader for Christ, which I guess is what he is supposed to be.

The way Theo was checking it out and rubbing his chin, I knew he was figuring how he'd look in those colors.

Everyone sat during the priest's sermon about immorality in modern American society. He personified this evil with the initials MM and BB as if saying the actual names of these movie harlots would summon the evil and taint the sanctity of the church. "My dear friends, you know who I'm talking about. I'll not defile the House of the Lord, nor contaminate the young impressionable minds at this morning's mass with the mention of their names."

"Who's he talking about?" Theo whispered.

I was surprised he was still listening. "Marilyn Monroe and Brigitte Bardot—you know, the actresses."

The sermon was the same age-old, sanctimonious intolerance. Rather than show any insight or shed wisdom on the faithful, the priest showed how out of touch he was with contemporary American life. Brigitte Bardot, the French sex-kitten, wasn't even an American. If it wasn't for the "condemned" movie list published each week in *The Michigan Catholic,* her movies would have been long forgotten by the average parishioner.

And the unfortunate Marilyn had been dead for five years. Isn't there a time-honored tradition of not speaking ill of the dead in church? The priest's sermon, to my mind, was beyond bad taste. I wonder if he would have maligned her had it been common knowledge at the time that she had been intimate with the most famous Catholic in America—John F. Kennedy.

As the offertory began, I motioned to Theo with a slight tug of my head to leave. We left while the ushers with their long-handled, satin-lined, wicker money baskets took care of their primary function, shilling for the parish. I thought of the old Irish saying, "He who sups with the devil should carry a long fork." We left before the ushers made it to the back of the church. I felt relieved when we hit the open morning air.

"That was really something," Theo said impressed.

"Yes, it was," I said. "The Catholic church has been in show business for a long time."

"What is it with you and religion?"

I was about to answer him when I stopped dead in my tracks. As we approached my car, there was a message for us: four slashed tires, each with a single puncture in the side wall. One tire, maybe an accident; four tires, an act of God. We looked around and didn't see a single soul. But we got the hell out of there. I hoped Theo had a better understanding of the realities of suburban life in the Detroit area.

"I'll pay for two of those tires," he offered.

"Thanks, I appreciate that, but you don't have to."

"But I'm goin' to," he insisted. Theo proved a good friend.

We got in the Bug and made our deflated getaway. With rubber slapping and walloping along the pavement as I drove, I momentarily forgot I was looking for a tire store open on a Sunday. I was thinking about the young redhead who winked at me in church.

After I had driven down Outer Drive Road for a couple of minutes without saying anything, Theo broke the silence. "What's on your mind, Jake?"

"Brigitte Bardot," I said without missing a beat.

11 Forbidden Fruit

After the parking-lot incident, we never spoke about going to church services together again. We worked as many double shifts as we were offered and didn't socialize beyond the occasional bite to eat at a sleazy diner outside of Zug Island. It was mid-June, and most of my college friends had returned home for summer vacation. I was still paying off my car and saving for tuition and books. I hadn't told Theo that the university had reinstated me for the fall semester as a probationary student. As much as I wanted to live on campus, staying at home was the wiser and more economical thing to do.

Theo hadn't heard from his wife or son in over two months. Whenever he tried to call Memphis, he couldn't connect with them. Usually, the phone rang unanswered, or if it was picked up, Doretha wasn't there. He sent several letters also but never knew if they had been delivered. It was clearly bothering him. Between double shifts one late afternoon, we walked over to the coal docks and sat down on the concrete embankment facing the river.

"Beautiful day today," I said.

"Huh?"

"Must not be much smog today. That blue sky goes on forever."

"Yeah."

"So, how's it going?"

Theo pulled a folded envelope from his work jacket. "I got this in the mail yesterday."

"What is it? A letter from home?"

"Not really … it's a divorce notice."

"Damn! I'm sorry to hear that." What else could I say? It sounded woefully inadequate, but it was the only response I had to offer.

"It's not your fault." He looked blankly across the river into Canada.

"At least you know where you stand now," I told him.

"How would that be?"

"Look at the bright side—when one door closes, another opens. Now you're free to shop around and look for someone else who wants to be with you."

"What makes you think I want someone else?"

"You're only twenty-three, for God's sake. I just thought—"

"I'm in no hurry to be tied down again. I was bound to Doretha for seven long years, Jake. That's a long damned time to be luggin' a ball and chain around."

"There must have been some good times too."

"Yeah, I just can't think of any."

I'd been neglecting Theo lately, so I thought it might cheer him up if we went out on the town again. Whatever spare time I had lately, I spent with my college friends, fresh home for the summer. I was drawn back to the suburbs and a future far removed from Zug Island. Preoccupied with my own life, I had no idea what Theo had been doing with his spare time.

"Hey, what do you say about hanging out this weekend?"

"And doing what?"

"Check out the talent! Cruise Woodward Avenue. I haven't had a date since last September when my girlfriend dumped me." The last bit of information sparked his attention.

"You never told me she dumped you."

"It wasn't important," I lied.

"Feels like shit, doesn't it?"

"Sure does. All I could do was sit in the basement and read."

"Read! That's where we're different, Jake. I gotta get out of the house. What was this gal's problem?"

I didn't want to reopen that wound, but if it took Theo's mind off his marital problems, it was the least I could do. "We went to different universities and drifted apart. That's all."

"She started fuckin' someone else, huh? I knew it!"

"I hate to disappoint you, but it wasn't like that. Sex wasn't the issue."

"Sex is always the issue. What's the matter with you, boy?"

"What do you mean, what's the matter with me? There's nothing the matter with me! Here I am trying to cheer up your sorry ass, and you're messing with me. I know about the pain of rejection. I know how you feel, that's all!"

"Was she good in bed?"

"Hell, I don't know! We never had sex." *Too much information!* Rather than letting the matter drop, it only encouraged him further and aggravated me more.

"Is it just you, or do all white boys start fuckin' so late?"

Now I was certain he was messin' with me. "Late? Shit! I don't know. I was taught to respect women. Sex is for marriage."

"I was thirteen the first time I got laid," he reminisced. "Her name was Lettie, and she was seventeen. I respected the hell out of Lettie. If she was here right now, I'd respect the hell out of her again."

"White girls want to get married first."

"Yeah, who told you that, your mother? You really believe that? How long did you go with this girl?"

"Why are you giving me the third degree? It's irrelevant." Being defensive was a mistake.

"How long, wuss?"

"A couple of years."

"A couple of years? You must've been doing something seriously wrong, mister," he said smirking.

"You're starting to piss me off now!"

"You don't have to be embarrassed."

"I'm not fucking embarrassed!"

"Eighteen and still a virgin. Christ almighty! I'd be embarrassed," he said shaking his head in disbelief. "I'll be goddamned."

"I don't doubt that."

"You ain't a faggot, are you?"

"Fuck you, Theo. I'm trying to cheer you up, and this is what I get? Give me a break, for Christ's sake!"

He burst out laughing.

"What's so damned funny?"

"You need a woman worse than I do."

"I'm glad I could be there for you."

"Thanks, I do feel better now," he said. "You crack me up sometimes!"

"Well? What about it? Does Friday night sound good?"

"Sounds good to me!"

I wasn't sure where we would go, but we'd figure that out later.

Friday night arrived, and I showed up on time. Theo wasn't ready, as usual. He'd be late to his own funeral. While I waited for him to spruce up, I looked at the entertainment section of the *Detroit Free Press.* My general plan was to catch a movie at one of the downtown theaters and maybe flirt with some young women. Down the hall in the community bathroom, I could hear Theo humming a rendition of the Four Tops song, "Baby I Need Your Loving." I read him some movie titles. There was a special showing of a Paul Newman film that I thought looked promising.

"I don't want to sit in some dark movie theater. No movie tonight," he said. "Alonzo gave me the good word on where to go."

"Oh, yeah. Where?"

Theo didn't answer but broke into a chorus of "Shop Around" by Smokey Robinson and the Miracles. "Now there is a good mother," he said alluding to the lyrics. "Don't be sold on the very first one. Pretty girls are a dime a dozen, better find one that'll give you good lovin'."

I was having second thoughts about the whole evening. Alonzo was a shady character, so my radar went up. "Well, what's the secret?"

"It's a surprise."

"I hate fucking surprises."

"I think you'll like this one," he said as we walked downstairs to the kitchen. The refrigerator door opened, and he brought out two quarts of Colt 45 Malt Liquor.

"I think I'll pass on that tonight."

"Pass on it, my ass! Relax. You're all uptight. Here, have some beer nuts with it," he insisted pushing the open package towards me. He popped the caps on the bottles with a church key. "This isn't that local piss water, Stroh's."

I took a short drink. He was right. This tasted thicker and stronger. "What's going down tonight?"

"Us, with any luck," he said disappearing up to his room and returning with a tray. "But first, you need to loosen up."

"What's this?"

"Reefer, man."

"Reefer?"

"Are you for real? Don't you know anything? You never heard of Mary Jane?"

"Marijuana—pot? I guess so. I never saw it before though."

"There's a first time for everything, my brother," he said taking a pinch from a baggie and crushing it between his thumb and forefingers onto a flat tray. "Smell this!" he said putting his fingers under my nose.

"Smells musty," I said sneezing. "Smoking isn't my thing. My parents used to chain smoke with the windows rolled up in the car whenever I rode with them. I hated the smell and vowed I would never be a smoker."

"Good boy," Theo said tilting the tray and shaking the seeds out from the rest of the pot and hand-rolling two joints from the cleaned product. "I got this lid from the Pinto Bean," he said holding up the baggie. "It's decent stuff. Not too many seeds and stems."

"I don't smoke. Really!"

"Suit yourself. Leaves more for me." Theo lit one, drew deeply, and held the smoke in for several moments, then exhaled in my face. The smoke hovered in the air and smelled pleasantly pungent. Different than tobacco. My curiosity was mildly aroused.

"How does it make you feel?"

When he finished his second hit, he answered, "It burns on one end, and irons you out on the other. Try some?"

"I don't want to get hooked. I've got enough problems."

"That's what I like about this shit. It doesn't solve your problems; it just softens 'em up." He blew another fog cloud at me; this time it smelled richer than before. I breathed more in. "It takes two people to keep it burning. A couple of tokes isn't going to hook anybody. Especially a nonsmoker like yourself." He offered it to me.

"You sure?"

"Sure, I'm sure!" he said.

"Pass it over then."

"Don't draw too hard on the first toke."

I didn't know what "too hard" was and coughed

my guts out. I gulped some beer to soothe my throat. Through watering eyes, I saw him smiling.

"Hand it back to me, damn it! See what I mean? It went out." He lit it again. "Take a shorter toke this time and hold it in."

This time I didn't cough. I slowly exhaled and felt relaxed after a few seconds or so. By the time we finished the joint, I didn't have a tense muscle in my body, and all felt right with the world.

"I'll take the other joint with us," he said putting it in with his pack of Kools. "You ready to cruise, bro'?"

"Just push me in the right direction," I said no longer caring where or what we were doing.

Theo and I cruised Woodward where he directed me to turn left after a few blocks and left again. We were in an area of rundown tenements. "Park on the side street and we'll walk from there."

We went half a block up the street and stopped at a rundown hotel.

"So this is the secret?"

"Señor Sanchez recommended this place," Theo said standing outside the Hotel Cleveland. "Let's go for it."

"Go for what?"

"Pussy, my man. Some of the fuzzy stuff."

"So this is your big secret!" I wondered how

many guys at the mill knew about this. Probably all of them.

"You're gonna get laid tonight," he said proudly as we walked up the stairs. I instantly sobered up. "Let me do the talkin'," he instructed.

I thought, *Good!* I was out of my element and my heart was pounding. I nodded "Okay!" and pulled at my crotch, rearranging my jock through my pants.

The lobby was as dingy as the secrets this fleabag hotel held. Behind the counter, a black clerk wearing a green eye shade was reading the evening edition of the *Detroit News*, while an exotic middle-aged woman, who looked Eurasian with her dark hair done up in a French twist, gave us the once-over. That's all she needed. She had determined we were no threat, so she resumed filing her nails. Theo tapped the desk bell once, and the clerk put his paper down. "What do you guys want?"

"A mutual friend sent me."

"Really! Does your friend have a name?"

Theo leaned forward and said, "Alonzo."

"Don't know him!"

"Alonzo Sanchez. He's a regular here."

"A regular what?" Right off the bat, it wasn't going well.

Anything connected with Alonzo was suspect. Just after I'd met him, he had pulled several bent photos from his billfold. "She looks pretty damned good. Don't she?" They were of a Latina woman, maybe in her mid-twenties. In poorly lit Polaroids, she struck several lewd poses. Her dark features and black hair matched her lingerie. I was immediately aroused. Against my better judgment, I asked, "Who is she?"

"She is my woman. Do you like her?" He said provocatively.

If I said "no," he might get angry. If I said "yes," I wasn't sure what I'd be getting myself into. I simply shrugged my shoulders saying nothing. My flushed cheeks had answered better than I could.

"What do you think?"

"Nice," I said understating my reaction. *She looked damned nice.*

"Well, my friend ... she's not for you. A young man like you could hurt himself with that. These photos, she does for me. You want to buy some?"

"I think I'll pass," seemed like a prudent response. I was so horny, I didn't need to buy them. They were etched on my mind.

Theo's voice drew me back to the present. "Our friend said we could possibly find a date here."

"Really?" The clerk said not volunteering any information. "This Alonzo talks a lot."

"What can I tell you? That's what he told me."

The clerk looked past him over to me. "Who's that guy playing with himself?"

Embarrassed, I took my hand out of my pocket and folded my arms.

"My young friend here is hoping to pop his cherry tonight. He's off to boot camp tomorrow morning."

That fool, Theo. I wanted to strangle the son of a bitch.

"What's that to me?" asked the clerk.

"Our friend, Alonzo—"

"That's okay, Frankie. I know Mr. Sanchez, the Cuban heel," the woman said looking up from her nails. The young one's kinda cute. It's all right!"

"So you're shipping out in the morning?" she asked, as if she was a concerned neighbor.

"Well, technically, I'm flying out," I lied.

"Anyway, our friend—" said Theo.

"Forget about your friend." The clerk held up his hand and rubbed his forefingers with his thumb. "Know anybody else?"

"Ever hear of Hamilton?" Theo said catching on quickly.

"I've heard of him, but he doesn't impress me much."

"What about Jackson?"

"Jackson is a friend of mine, but Grant is like a brother to me."

I didn't know about Theo, but I didn't have fifty bucks. This wasn't how I imagined my first sexual experience would go. I felt like Holden Caulfield. I didn't want to have his same experience—he went to a tenement hotel to buy sex, didn't get laid, was robbed, and got punched in the face for his troubles.

"What about two Jacksons?"

The clerk looked back at the lady now sitting with her arms and legs crossed. She nodded saying, "Two Jacksons will do. It's a slow night."

"For the both of us?"

"Get the fuck out of here!" the clerk snapped. "You're wasting my goddamn time."

"Okay! Be cool! How about a Hamilton and a Jackson apiece?"

The clerk pulled a snub nosed revolver from under the counter. I had been quiet so far but that ended when I saw the gun. "We'll be going now," I said tugging on Theo's arm as I backed him towards the door.

Safely out on the street, I started bitching at him. "Are you nuts? I'm not willing to get shot over a piece of ass. Let's get the hell out of here."

"I'm comin' back here with more money next time."

"You'll be coming by yourself then!"

"I've been doing plenty of that lately."

"Very funny."

Suddenly, I was hungry. We jumped in the car and picked up some sliders and fries at the first White Castle we saw, and Theo picked up a couple of Mickey's Malt Liquors from a nearby party store. I drove to Grand

Circus Park where we ate while planning our next move.

Detroit's Hookers' Alley ran along John R. and Brush which was only a few blocks north from where we were. My eunuch high school friends and I would occasionally buzz the prostitutes, hooting and hollering with no intention of getting laid. It was something for idiot white kids from the suburbs to do on boring evenings. I suggested we cruise Brush St. to check it out. At least I knew what to expect there.

It was Friday night and the street was hopping. People milled around the entrances of several nightclubs where live blues and jazz music poured out as we cruised past. The traffic flowed constantly around the several blocks of Detroit's red-light district. There were ghetto cruisers, pimp mobiles, taxis, and gawkers like us. My yellow VW was the oddest-looking thing on the street.

I turned the corner to cruise John R. St. and saw a wolf pack of eight to ten working girls on the street corner. It was the nightly parade of erotic vagrants, each lady provocatively dressed: one had on a blue sequined, extremely short dress; another wore a red satin Suzie Wong dress with a slit up the leg; a couple of the girls had on leather shorts and low-cut blouses with push-up bras; still another had on a leopard jumpsuit and a purple wig. What they all wore in common were "fuck me" pumps in an array of eye-catching colors. As luck would have it, the stoplight turned red before we could get through the intersection. Theo was like a kid in a candy store.

Several of the girls left the curb and approached my car. It was a hot and stuffy evening, so my windows were rolled down, which to their way of thinking identified us as players. Theo leaned across me, throwing out a come-on to them. "What's shakin', pretty mamas?"

"Hey, baby! Want some?" one of the ladies shouted pushing her buxom breasts together.

"Oh, my goodness gracious. Look at those tits!" he said to me.

All I could manage to say was, "Holy shit."

Another of the ladies lifted her dress, revealing a black garter belt and red silk panties. "This could be all yours, lover," she said, rubbing herself.

I wondered why these girls came forward and not the others; I figured that they must rotate like at a taxi stand. From the curb, they looked exotic; from two feet away, they looked rugged and dangerous.

"What's goin' on, ladies?" Theo began.

"You and me baby, if the price is right," said the lead hooker.

"I'll take the apple-cheeked one," said the woman in the blond Marilyn wig and green eye shadow. "You look brand-new, honey. Wanna bump uglies with me tonight?" She reached into the car and rubbed between my legs. "What do you say? Let's me and you do the mattress dance. You feel like you're just about ready to me."

I didn't answer. I was about to cream my jeans.

"How much?" Theo asked. The bargaining began.

"Depends what you want, darlin'."

"It all looks good," Theo said stroking his goatee. "How much, momma?"

"We've got a special on blowjobs tonight, just for you. Twenty for one; thirty for two."

"Sounds like a bargain, don't it?" he said to me.

Before any money passed hands, the traffic light turned green. Much to Theo's disappointment, I hit the gas and wound out first gear, leaving the ladies behind cursing us. "What's up with that, Jake? Are you crazy? Go back!"

"No can do, Kemo Sabe!" I said looking into my rearview mirror.

"Why the hell not?"

"A squad car pulled out from the alley and the ladies scattered everywhere. We're lucky to get out of there."

"Damn it! This car is a cop magnet," Theo said.

"The squad car turned up John R. St."

"Well, I'm comin' back here too!"

It was getting to be eleven thirty, and I'd had enough excitement for one night. We didn't accomplish what we set out to do, but we managed to stave off boredom and get Theo's mind off his wife. That was worth something.

"Are you thirsty?"

"Naw, but I do need to take a leak," I told him.

"Turn down one of these alleys and we'll piss behind a dumpster."

After two large beers and as many unfulfilled hard-ons, I had to relieve myself soon or pee my pants. I managed to pull into an alley not a second too soon. As bad as I had to go, it came out in a slow trickle. Theo pissed like a fire hose and was finished in no time.

Walking back to the car, he heard the familiar rattle of dice and looked down the alley. Three guys were playing craps in a dimly lit delivery entrance. We hadn't spent much money this evening, so Theo took fifty dollars from his billfold and folded the bills lengthwise and wrapped them around the knuckle of his index finger. "Lock my wallet in your car. Ever play craps?" he asked.

"Not really. I'm more of a coin tosser."

"Well, I've got my lucky shirt on. Watch the master."

I locked my car and followed him into the alley, thinking I should have my head examined. But he did snooker me at pool, so this might work out after all.

"Is this game open?" Theo said as he waded deeper into the alley.

The three men looked over their shoulders and wondered what to make of us. "Five dollar minimum. Can you handle that?"

"I'm in!" Theo said.

"What about your friend?"

"He's not a gambler."

"He's not your sissy boy, is he?" said one of the gamblers who was wearing a sleeveless undershirt, plaid shorts, and flip-flops.

Everybody had a good laugh at my expense. I was wearing an Izod polo shirt and a pair of Levis that must have looked queer to them. Theo came to my defense. "No, it's not like that."

I stayed safely in the background. If it had been a card game, they would have objected, but with craps, it didn't matter. Besides, they controlled the dice. The poorest of the men had more money clenched in his fist than Theo had around his finger, in his wallet, and tucked in the toe of his shoe. He must have smelled of loose money because it took less than fifteen minutes to clean him out, including his shoe money. Seventy or eighty bucks was my guess. He was having a bad night; even Lady Luck had deserted him. I almost felt sorry for the poor sucker.

"Lend me some money," he asked.

I only had forty bucks on me. "Here's a twenty. That's all I have," I told him. He went up and down with each roll of the dice for five more minutes before he was broke again. But he wanted to play more; he needed to play more.

"Hey, bro', you can't play if you don't pay," the tee-shirt model said.

"I hear you, man. What do you give me for this watch?"

"I don't want your watch, man."

"How about you?" Theo said to one of the other shooters. "It's a seventeen-jewel Bulova." He took it off his wrist and held it out for closer examination. "My wife got it for me."

"How much?"

"Fifty."

"Forget it!"

"Forty." The man ignored him.

"Thirty. It's almost brand-new. I got it for Christmas."

"Twenty," said the dishwasher, wearing a grimy apron, who had stepped out for a smoke and a few throws of the dice on his break behind the restaurant.

"Sold," said Theo. The money was exchanged and the wristwatch went onto the man's arm. I hoped he washed dishes and didn't cook in that filthy apron.

Another ten minutes went by and we were on the road again, predictably no wiser but broker. I thought Theo would be angry, but he pulled out a cigarette. "This is the best time I've had since I've been in Detroit," he said with satisfaction.

"Don't mention it," I said surprised.

If the truth be known, I also had a good time, but I didn't want to encourage him further. His spirit impressed me. I wondered what wellspring of optimism he drew from so I could drink deeply from it too. He had been deserted by his wife, he was an unwilling party to a divorce procedure and was certainly going to lose his son, he had been shut down twice for booty, and he lost everything but his lucky gambling shirt tonight in that alley. Either he was the most easygoing person I had ever met, or he was one brass-plated buffoon.

While I drove along, Theo lit up the joint he had saved. I didn't like the idea of him smoking anything in my car, especially reefer, so the first chance I got, I pulled onto a side street and found a darkened alley. We got out and finished the rest of it.

"Now, what do you want to do? It's your turn," he said.

"We can still make the 10:00 PM showing of that movie I wanted to see earlier this evening." This time he didn't protest. We drove across town to the Livernois and Davidson area looking for a movie theater called the Studio One, which showed art films.

The theater had a special showing of a Paul Newman film, *The Outrage,* I'd heard about from a movie-buff friend of mine. Newman's films were generally more mainstream than this Western adaptation of the classic Japanese movie, *Rashomon*. The film was too sophisticated for the general public and didn't do great at the box office the first time around, but it had a second life on the art theater circuit. I was hoping that we could stay out of trouble and kill a couple of hours watching a good movie together.

"What's it about?"

"The nature of truth," I said thinking he might squawk, but he didn't. My theory was he needed to sit down someplace for awhile. I still had the twenty I held back from the crap game. I told him I was broke earlier, but he either forgot or didn't care—such is the nature of truth sometimes.

The Studio One's parking lot was full on this Saturday night, so I reluctantly headed for a side street and found a space two short blocks away. We had only about ten minutes or so until the feature started, and I hate to be late for anything, so I started to walk briskly. Theo, on the other hand, wouldn't ask the time of day from a watch, especially when it was now on someone else's wrist. He was happy and carefree, sauntering along with a self-confident stroll. He didn't care if we missed the coming attractions or opening credits. After dragging me through an evening of some of Detroit's meanest streets, he conceded to do something I wanted to do, see a movie. What could go wrong?

I waited for him to catch up to me. "Do you like going to the movies?" I asked him.

"I just been a couple of times."

"Really?" That surprised me because when I was growing up, I went to the Saturday afternoon matinees almost every weekend with a group of neighborhood kids. Those were the days when the theaters were still running movie serials from the 1930s and 1940s in addition to a cartoon and a double feature. It wasn't until I was a teenager that I figured out my mom and dad needed that time alone.

"We used to go weekly and throw popcorn at the girls," I mentioned to Theo as we approached the box office.

"Do I have to sit upstairs?"

"What?"

"In the South, negros sit upstairs while whites sit downstairs."

"Hell, no! What about your civil rights? That's against the law now."

"Well, old habits die hard in some places, my friend."

"Don't worry. There's no balcony here. We can sit wherever we want," I said. "Is that why you didn't go to the movies much as a kid?"

"Naw! Poor black folks can't waste money on movies; besides, they were always about white people."

Suddenly, he pulled me from behind by the belt loop of my Levis and almost gave me a walking whiplash; then, he deftly stepped in front of me. "What the fuck!" I said.

"Hey, Jake! Do you see what I see?" Theo was standing with his back to the box office. He motioned with his head for me to look over his left shoulder. Without looking, I knew already what it was about.

"Did I see what?" Then, I turned my head and saw her. Sitting inside the ticket booth was a great-looking young woman with blonde hair, maybe in her early twenties, reading a paperback book. It's hard to judge someone's age from fifteen feet away through a box office window at night while looking over someone's shoulder.

Theo apparently didn't have that problem. He had already surmised her weight, cup size, and natural pubic coloration. "You are certifiable," I told him.

He didn't understand the reference. "What you talking about?"

"She's sitting down. How can you tell the color of her pubic hair you crazy idiot?" I smirked.

"Her eyebrows, fool." The surety of his quick answer made me suspect he was right. "She's got the look. I'm telling you!"

"What look? Come on, we're gonna be late. We've only got five minutes. Let's buy our tickets, grab a seat, and watch this goddamned movie."

Theo stopped dead in his tracks, pursed his lips, and shook his head. "How are you ever going to meet a woman? You want to die a virgin?"

"I've just had enough excitement for one evening," I said copping out.

"I thought you wanted to get laid tonight."

"No! You wanted me to get laid tonight." We quibbled as we walked towards the box office. I looked up at the ticket lady and opened my mouth to say,

"One, please," but nothing came out. When we made eye contact, I blew a fuse because I was looking at her eyebrows and all my mind's eye could see was her golden triangle. A rush of animal magnetism made a mute of me and froze me to the spot.

Theo, who was prodding me from behind, brushed past and said flashing his gold tooth, "Two, darlin.' How are you doing this fine evening?"

"I'm doing fine. That will be ten dollars please."

I just stood there. "Pay the lady, Jake." He nudged me. I forgot I had the cash and slid a twenty through the window opening. Theo grabbed the tickets and the ten dollars change. "You'll have to excuse my friend, pretty lady. He's hypnotized by your beauty and wants to date you."

With that, the spell was broken. I tried to grab his arm to drag him away before humiliating me any further, but he spun free. "I can vouch for him. He's a nice guy, but he's too shy to ask you for your phone number, baby."

I blanked out for a second or two when I heard her say, "Really?" My face flushed and my head was about to explode from my rising blood pressure. It was only the erection in my pants that kept my eyeballs from popping out. The beautiful young woman turned her head and looked at me with understanding eyes. After a slight pause, she said, "Wait a minute," through the voice hole in the ticket booth window. The blonde jotted down her phone number on the inside of a matchbook cover for me. She motioned with one raised eyebrow and a slight nod of her head for me to come back to the ticket booth where I almost lost it again. She closed the cover over the matches and slid them out the window. All I could think to say was, "Thank you."

"Call me early in the afternoon sometime," she said showing an interest that surprised me and Theo.

I became lightheaded, and my heart beat out a happy tune. Rather than harangue Theo about embarrassing me in front of a woman, I felt like thanking him. His crude instincts had opened a door for me, and for the first time, I saw that he was slightly envious. Served him right for embarrassing me. We entered the movie theater, and I smelled the popcorn.

12

The Laying on of Hands

The water in the backyard pool was still as a plate-glass window and just as transparent. Walt Dunwoody and I had been friends since before junior high school, and I had grown up in his family's pool. At the moment, I was content sitting under an umbrella-covered patio table drinking a highball on the rocks and munching from a bowl of salted mixed nuts. Walt picked around the Brazil nuts. "I don't eat the nigger toes."

"I don't mind them," I said popping one into my mouth.

"That's what I gather from what you've been telling me."

"Smooth, Walt. Smooth."

"Does your mother know what you've been up to since you've been working at that place?"

"She asks me no questions, and I tell her no lies."

"Right! She'd freak out if she knew you were cruising the ghetto with your coon buddy."

"Why worry the poor woman?" I said hoping to squelch the subject.

"I've seen your mother go to work on you, Jake, and it's not a pretty sight."

"What's your point?"

"Nothing, I'm just saying," Walt said letting it drop. "Did you ever call that ticket taker back?" he cross-examined.

"Yeah, but she wrote down a fake phone number."

"Think she was playing you?"

"No, I don't think so. She saw how Theo was prodding and pushing me and how I was squirming. She threw me a bone. I don't know why. Maybe she was trying to humor me. Whatever her reason, it was sweet."

"Sweet? Why don't you go back there and bonk her? You know where she works."

"No, I don't think so."

"You gonna have a green weenie for the rest of your life?"

Now I was getting the same business from Walt I had been getting from Theo. These guys were more alike than Walt would have been comfortable admitting. "I noticed a wedding band on her left hand," I said.

"Even better. Experience without commitment."

"Stalking a married woman isn't my style, dude."

"Don't get self-righteous with me, Mr. Clean. Let's change the subject!"

"Suits me fine."

"So, Mr. Lincoln ... how did you like the movie?" That was Walt's feeble attempt at humor. He was a pre-law student at the University of Michigan, home from Ann Arbor for the summer, languishing in the lap of luxury. We both loved the movies, and he had recommended *The Outrage* to me because it was, among other things, a courtroom drama that plays out in front of a burned-out courthouse in New Mexico.

"Theo fell asleep and was snoring fifteen minutes into it." I laughed. "So I moved down a couple of rows to hear better. It's a great film. I especially liked Claire Bloom's performance, the innocent flower but the serpent underneath," I said quoting Shakespeare poorly. Luckily, Walt wasn't an English major and thought I came up with that myself.

"Well put. You've always been quick with a quip. I'm glad you're getting out of that hellhole before it rots your mind," he said as he mixed himself another drink.

"It's not so bad. Another six or seven weeks, and I'll be done with it," I said.

"You're going to work until the bitter end, huh?"

"I gots ta make dat money, bro'."

"Christ! I don't know how you've stood it for this long. You're even starting to sound like them."

Walt had never worked a day in his life, unless

you consider kissing his father's ass a full-time job. In return, his father provided a safe and sheltered environment with a heated pool and an assured future in his father's advertising firm.

"Some of us have to work for a living. Besides, there are some real characters and good people on Zug Island that I wouldn't have met anyplace else."

"What's that guy's name again?"

I took a sip from my drink. "Theo Semple."

"With a name like 'Simple,' he must be one dumb jungle bunny."

"It's 'Semple,' you shithead! Don't call him a jungle bunny or a coon or a nigger in front of me, okay? He's my friend. Respect that." I tossed up a Brazil nut and caught it in midair to emphasize the point.

Walt was letting his pre-law major go to his head. "Jake, look at the facts. He can't get laid in a whorehouse with a pocket full of fifty dollar bills. He loses his watch in a back-alley craps game. He strikes out with streetwalkers on Brush St. Come on, the guy's a loser! Get real!" Walt swirled the ice in his glass and downed the rest of his drink as if he had made his point. "Case closed!"

Working a swing shift for six months, I was able to watch a lot of daytime television, and *Perry Mason* was among my favorite shows. I couldn't wait for an opening to use Mason's patented objection, "That's irrelevant, immaterial, and incompetent," to trounce Walt's bigoted arguments. It wasn't Shakespeare, but the quote had a certain ring to it, and I was certain he wouldn't recognize it.

"He's a good guy. I guess you had to be there," I continued. "Sometimes, he's pretty damned quick."

"For example?" was Walt's quick rejoinder. Putting people on the defensive was Walt's favorite debating technique. I knew he would put me on the spot whenever he could, so I was ready.

"We had just finished our shift last week, and this Cuban guy everyone calls the Pinto Bean comes up to Theo and starts stroking Theo's goatee and says, 'Your beard feels like my woman's pussy.' Without missing a beat, Theo rubs his chin and says, 'You know? I think you're right.'"

Walt laughed, "That is pretty fast."

I knew he'd like that story on the face of it.

"Everyone in the lunchroom cracked up, including Alonzo. That takes a quick wit to turn something around like that."

"I'll grant you this; the guy sounds like a character. I've had enough of this working-class hero bullshit. How about a Tom Collins this time?" he said.

"Give me another Seven and Seven. It's going down easy, but lighten up on the Seagrams."

He went over to the poolside cabana bar and threw together a couple more drinks. "When Sherry and her girlfriend get here, I'll make some Rum and Coke. Chicks love those."

"I'll stick with what I'm drinking. It upsets my stomach to mix drinks."

"Christ, you're a lightweight."

"I'm not much of a drinker these days."

"Smokin' de marijuana, hey, man?"

"Seems harmless enough."

"Unless you get busted. I'm sticking with booze. Liquor is quicker."

"Speaking of booze, where are your parents this weekend?" I asked, trying to divert the subject away from Theo and me.

"They're spending the Fourth of July with friends at the Elmwood Casino. They're probably having an orgy or something. Who cares? They're out of my hair for a couple of days."

"Why are they in Canada on Independence Day?"

"The fireworks are better against the Detroit skyline than with Windsor in the background," he said bringing me my drink. "You've never been over there to see them?"

"Never been to Canada."

"Christ, you are deprived," he said with mock pity.

"Your old man is gonna freak out when he finds out we're drinking his liquor," I said.

"He'll never know the difference. Believe me. You worry more than my old Aunt Agnes."

"Yeah, right! That's what you said before he caught us watching his porno films and flipped out."

If Walt wasn't worried about it, I decided not to be either. His parents entertained a lot. Walt's father was an advertising executive who used the pool as a prop for TV commercials and print ads enough to deduct it as a business expense. He knew how to work the tax angles.

One afternoon while I was hanging out at their house, he told Walt, "Son, get a job where you don't have to get your hands dirty. You can judge a man by his fingernails." That snobby-assed attitude pissed me off because I was the offspring of generations of men who weren't afraid to get their hands dirty. My father could have snapped that pencil-necked geek's manicured hand off his wrist with one handshake.

"I couldn't believe what Lynette did to you, man. She didn't give you any warning?"

"Just a phone call … and I made that." The conversation shifted back to me, but it was better than listening to Walt's racist attitudes.

"How did she tell you it was over?"

"Pretty much stuff like: 'It's over. Don't call me anymore. I don't want to hurt you. We've grown apart.' You know, bullshit like that."

"Ouch!"

"I'm pretty much over it now and better off."

"Fucking-A straight! Especially after you meet Brooke."

That was the object of this pool party. Walt and his girlfriend were going to fix me up. I was their charity case. Despite feeling awkward, I had nothing better to do, and the alcohol helped. "Tell me about her."

"Brooke's a stone fox."

"You've already told me that. What about her?"

"She just graduated from Our Lady of Grace—"

"Damn, another Catholic!"

"There you go, being negative again. Lighten up, for Christ's sake!"

"I've had my fill of professional virgins. Lynette strung me out for over two years."

"Lynette was a bitch! Brooke isn't like that. Her boyfriend dumped her last month, so she's licking her wounds."

"On the rebound? Finally, some useful information. What else?"

"The guy shipped back to Nam after a re-enlistment leave. He took her to her prom, and he put some aggressive moves on one of her friends. They argued, and he told her to go fuck herself."

"That's pretty harsh. We have rejection in common, anyway."

"No kidding! Sherry and I thought you two would be a good match."

"A couple of losers on the rebound, huh?"

"Beggars can't be choosy, buddy."

"The next thing you'll be telling me is she has a nice personality." I was feeling worse as the minutes passed. "Describe her for me again. This time use some adjectives."

"She has—" Several light taps on the backyard gate interrupted him. "See for yourself," he said approaching the wooden security gate.

Sherry entered first and put her arms around Walt's shoulders and gave him a full-body hug and a deep kiss. "I see you've started without us. Hello, Jake!" she said waving to me.

Damn, Sherry looked good! Then Brooke entered the yard. She was wearing a white terrycloth tunic revealing a black bikini underneath, and she had on dark sunglasses and a broad-brimmed sun hat that made her look like a fashion model. I couldn't believe my eyes and almost choked on a peanut. She was the girl from church, the one with the auburn hair.

"How you doing, sweetheart?" Walt said putting his arm around her waist and kissing her behind the ear.

I rose from the patio chair and greeted Sherry with a polite hug.

"Jake, this is my dear friend, Brooke."

I smiled and said, "Nice to meet you … again."

"We've met?" Brooke asked.

"Sort of."

She tilted her head but couldn't remember me. "Refresh my memory."

"I saw you at church a couple of months ago." I hoped that might jog her memory. "You were with your grandmother, I believe."

"I'm sorry, but I don't remember."

"I was with the black guy."

"Oh, yes! I remember now."

"Hi. My name's Jake," I said extending my hand and feeling like a jerk.

Walt rescued me. "Rum and Cokes, ladies?"

"We'd love some." Sherry smiled as they sat down.

I followed Walt to the bar. He mixed the drinks, and I opened a bag of chips and grabbed a bowl of dip. "What do you think?"

"She looks great. Now I really feel like a dork."

"Relax! She's easy to talk with," he coached.

"So you're going back to Eastern in the fall," Brooke said as I returned with the snacks.

"That's right! I'm really looking forward to it. I'll be commuting this time around."

"Is that your yellow Beetle parked out front?"

"Yes, it is."

"It's cute. I like it."

"Thanks."

"Brooke has been accepted at U of D," Sherry said.

"University of Detroit. That's great!"

"I'm pretty excited about it."

"What's your major?" Even before the words came out, I thought, *Could I be more predictable?*

"Nursing, I guess. I'm not sure yet."

Walt brought over a pitcher of iced Rum and Cokes for the girls. They each drank two rounds before I finished my highball. The drinks oiled our tongues and made the conversation flow. After a while, Walt maneuvered Sherry inside the house, leaving Brooke outside with me.

"Do you want to swim?" I asked her.

"Eventually." She removed her tunic, revealing beautifully tanned shoulders. The rest of her looked pretty damn good too.

I took off my tropical shirt revealing my worker's tan. My job didn't allow much time for sunbathing. My torso and legs looked like I had been hiding under a rock someplace. I tried to scrub as much of the coal residue off as I could in the shower; I hoped she wouldn't notice. "I haven't had much time to sunbathe and even out my tan," I said mocking myself.

"Oh, my! You certainly have a muscular build though."

"Thanks. It's one of the benefits of my job."

"What do you do?"

"I make steel."

"Fascinating," she said reaching into her bag and taking out a tube of Coppertone. "Would you do my back?"

"Yeah, sure," I said, almost swallowing my tongue. She turned her back to me, pulling her shoulder-length hair off her neck with both hands, lifting her breasts together and revealing some heavenly cleavage. I squeezed the Coppertone tube and a white dollop of lotion came out with a sputter in my hand. *Be cool,* I told myself. I spread it evenly along her shoulders while my blood pressure rose. The touch of her skin and the smell of the suntan lotion intoxicated me.

"Who's your black friend?" she asked, breaking the spell.

What? I thought. *I can't get away from him.* "Just a guy I work with."

"Really? Who is he?"

She seemed more interested in him than me.

"Theo is his name."

"Where do you guys work?"

"Zug Island." While rubbing lotion on her back, the last thing I wanted to talk about was my damned job.

"Where's that?"

"Just off Delray in south Detroit."

"Sounds dynamic."

"Believe me, it's not."

"Would you like me to do your back?" she said lowering her arms.

"Sure, it's tough to reach by myself."

"Tell me about it," she said smearing the lotion up and down my spine. Nothing had ever felt so good.

"Just graduated, huh?"

"Yeah, from Our Lady of Grace. I'm glad to be done with Catholic high school. The people there are so narrow. I'm looking forward to going to an integrated school."

"True, but why a Catholic college? Why not a state college?"

"They gave me a scholarship."

"U of D has a good reputation. Are you living at home?"

"For the first semester anyway. My folks aren't ready to have me move out yet. They don't trust me." *Wonderful,* I thought.

"The first semester can be pretty tough. I found that out the hard way."

"Sherry told me."

"Good, because I'm tired of talking about it. Speaking of Sherry, where are those two?"

"They're banging each other's brains out by now."

She surprised me when she said that, and I didn't respond.

"This Rum and Coke isn't agreeing with me," Brooke said. "Walt makes them too darned strong. Would you get me a plain Coke, please?"

"Sure, I'll see if he has any more."

When I returned, she had a lighter and a joint on the table. "My ex-boyfriend left me this before he shipped out. It's Vietnamese."

What? I thought. *This sheltered Catholic girl smokes pot? I'll be damned.*

"You look shocked."

"Do you want me to be?"

"Maybe a little," she smiled coyly.

The joint was huge and packed into a cigarette skin. She lit it and took a hit; then she passed it over to me. After a couple of tokes, I said, "This is some good shit."

"My fool ex-boyfriend left behind what remains from a pack of these. I've got about three or four joints left."

"I've never seen anything like this," I said admiring how perfectly rolled it looked.

"In Vietnam, they make them look like cigarettes and sell it in Lucky Strike packs. My boyfriend brought a whole carton back with him."

"No kidding? I'd like to get some of this."

"Sorry, I can't get anymore. He's back in Nam."

"Man, this is good stuff. You should break them up and roll them into smaller joints though. Smoking it like this just wastes it."

"How do you feel?" she asked.

"I'm really stoned."

"This stuff really loosens me up."

"Really?" I asked looking into her hazel eyes.

"Really."

Cautiously, I reached for her hand and slowly drew her to me. We drifted into a prolonged embrace of soft moist kisses. "Want to swim?" I asked after some time.

"No," she said, leading me into the pool.

This was more than I could have hoped for as the water lapped to our own syncopated rhythm.

It had been three weeks since the pool party. Brooke and I had spent as much time together as my work and her parents would allow. We went to see a couple of movies and shacked up at my house when my mother went to work at the florist shop. I was burning the candle at both ends and having the time of my life.

That didn't leave much time for Theo. I hadn't mentioned Brooke to him because he'd grill me about her. Who is she? How'd you meet her? Have you done it? How is she? Why didn't you tell me about her? He was worse than a crime reporter. What I dreaded most was that I knew he would ask me to fix him up with one of her friends. I didn't need that aggravation. It was easier not to tell him anything. In another month or so, he and Zug Island would be fading memories for me.

Theo wasn't overly concerned that we hadn't hung out much. Without me for an anchor, he navigated past the desk clerk at the Hotel Cleveland and became a regular there. He told me he knew several of the ladies personally, and he would put in a good word for me the next time we were there.

"I've got that place wired, Jake!"

"No thanks!"

"What's the problem?"

"It's just not my thing," I insisted.

"What? Your thing's not workin'?" He stared sideways at me sensing something had changed, but he couldn't put his finger on it.

"What?" I said.

"I don't know. Something's different." He was puzzled. Watching him trying to figure me out was amusing. It hadn't occurred to him that I might be able to meet a woman without his help.

Payday was coming up, and we had Saturday night off. I thought we might take one last loop through the city before I quit my job and got my life back on track. Other than my French credits, I had earned twelve semester credits for the fall term, so I wasn't beginning from ground zero. It seemed like one last night out on the town with Theo was in order.

I bought some Mexican pot from Alonzo, mostly seeds and stems, and spent the early evening with Brooke getting high and listening to records. Her supply of grass had run out. My mom was visiting her sister in Port Huron for the week, so I had full run of the house. After we showered, I took her home before her nine o'clock curfew and picked Theo up a little later than usual, at about ten.

The evening was sweltering, so I dressed in an open-collared, loose shirt, a pair of camel linen pants, and leather huaraches. I was learning how to dress. For once, Theo was ready and sitting on the porch waiting for me. Everyone was sitting on their porches to beat the heat. We drove into downtown and parked near the Bob Lo dock, but we were too late to catch the boat to the island amusement park. Even the breeze off the river was sticky and died of suffocation when it brushed against us. We went to an all-night diner and ordered a couple of ice-cold lemonades that Theo spiked with Mohawk lime vodka. Despite being miserably hot, I ordered a foot long and some fries because I had a bad case of the munchies.

"You sure about the Cleveland? My treat!"

"It's not about the money. I'm just not interested."

"Not interested in pussy! What's got into you?"

I used one of his tactics and simply shrugged my shoulders. I could tell it hurt his feelings that I wouldn't let him treat me to a woman, so the time came to tell him about Brooke. "It wouldn't be fair to my lady."

"I knew it!" he exclaimed like his number had just come in.

"You didn't have a clue."

"Shit! I knew there was something different about you," he said grinning from ear-to-ear. He seemed happier about it than I was. "When did you meet her?"

I knew the rest of the questions, so I rattled off the answers, "Her name is Brooke; I met her over the Fourth of July holiday…"

"I wondered why you didn't work the Fourth of July. Passin' up double time and a quarter wasn't like you."

"And we've been an item ever since," I finished.

"What the fuck does that mean? An item! Are you getting laid?"

"She wore me out earlier this evening."

"I'll be goddamned! What does she look like?"

I was even prepared for that question. "Well, she's kind of hard to describe." I took the graduation photo Brooke had given me out of my wallet and showed it to him. The waitress brought me my foot long. I was starving.

"She's a looker, all right," he said stroking his goatee like a satyr.

"You know how senior pictures are. They're all touched up."

He examined the photo closely.

"What's the matter?" I knew what it was, but I enjoyed watching him trying to figure it out.

"She looks familiar."

I covered my fries with ketchup and started eating. "That's what you say about all the ladies," I pointed out between bites.

"Where did you meet her?"

"She's the girl who winked at me in church."

"You've got to be shitting me."

"I don't think so."

After I told him, he quit pressing me about getting laid. We finished my fries, got in the Bug, and moved on. Alonzo had told Theo about a part of town called The Turf that he wanted to check out. I hadn't been there, so we headed north on Woodward Avenue, turned left on West Grand Boulevard, and turned right when we got to 12th Street. It was close to midnight, and the street was at full throttle, in contrast to my neighborhood where almost everyone was asleep by now.

Predictably, Theo wanted to stop, so I parked in the first spot I found. He took a slug of vodka and offered me some. I waved it off.

"You're not game for anything, tonight."

"I'm spent, but don't let me slow you down."

In the time it took to make my excuse, a lanky black prostitute wearing lime green pedal pushers and a calypso blouse approached my car, looking for some action. Her slick-haired pimp was standing against a building, keeping a wary eye on his goods.

Theo opened with his standard come-on, "How you doing, pretty momma?"

"You boys looking for a good time?" she said, looking into my car.

"You know," he said stroking his goatee.

"Time is money, boys. You wanna party or what?"

This passion play wasn't sitting well with me. "Just him, not me!" I said.

"What's a matter? Too hot for you?"

"Hell no! I'm a steelworker," I said proudly.

"Well, that's good news, anyway. You guys just got paid." Then she turned her attention to Theo. "How about you, sweet cheeks?" She knew he was interested because he couldn't keep the drool off his beard.

"That depends. What's on the menu, darling?"

"How much do you want to spend?" she said playing along.

They were taking too much time. I could see

her pimp getting edgy. I wished Theo would cut the bullshit and get on with it.

"Tell me what you've got."

"Straight leg for twenty, head and tail for thirty. What's it gonna be, lover?"

"Close the deal," I said.

"How much for some head?"

"For you, sugar, fifteen dollars."

"Hop in and we'll go some place quiet."

"In this?" She said pointing to my Bug. "You must be jokin'."

"You don't have to hurt my friend's feelings."

"I've got a room up the block. Follow me!"

"What about your watchdog?" This was the first note of caution I had ever heard from Theo.

"He's my banker. Grease the man's palm when you pass by him."

"What if he follows?"

"He won't! It's bad for business."

Theo could resist anything but temptation. It was clear to me that he would follow her.

"If her pimp starts to follow, I'll beep my horn," I reassured him.

He took a twenty dollar bill out of his billfold and left his ID and remaining cash under the seat. He folded and palmed the bill; then, he got out of the car. Before he made the transaction, three vice cops materialized from nowhere, and a squad car suddenly appeared and skidded to a stop on the wrong side of the street. The biggest cop pushed Theo up against the wall with his nightstick while the other two went for the woman. Her pimp stood by impassively while the cops wrestled with her. He was a businessman all right. One of the cops caught her by the wrist, but she twisted and broke free. The other cop lost his balance trying to block her escape. The prostitute ran down the street quicker than Wilma Rudolph; then she vanished.

A small crowd started harassing the cops, led on by the girl's pimp. This neighborhood was used to raids born out of long experience dealing with the hard-nosed Detroit police department. A scene had developed as was the nature of the volatile street culture. The cop detaining Theo rushed to the aid of his fellow officers while the cop in the squad car radioed for backup. Things were happening so fast that Theo took his opportunity, slipped away unnoticed, and jumped in the VW. I slammed the stick into first gear, pulled onto 12th St., and rushed through a yellow light at the intersection. We were out of there just as we heard the approaching police sirens from the Livernois, 10th Precinct Station, and we escaped down the street. The cops were zero for two.

"That's enough excitement for one night," I told Theo.

"Yeah. That was a close one."

I sped down West Grand Boulevard, left on Chicago, and headed to the Jeffries Freeway. Almost getting arrested did more to arouse Theo than sober him up. He still wanted to swing by the Cleveland, but I discouraged him. "Naw, I'm tired and it's late. Let's call it a night."

Reluctantly, he agreed. I dropped him off and drove home. I was worn out, and it felt good to slip into bed knowing I still had a few days off to rest before I had to return to work. But the next morning brought some surprising and disturbing news: Detroit was burning.

13 What Fools We Humans Be

On *Sunday morning, July* 23, 1967, I was trying to catch up on lost sleep when the phone rang just after seven o'clock in the morning. I figured my mother was checking up on me from Port Huron where she was visiting my aunt, so I let it ring five times before I answered it with a drowsy, "Good morning."

"You're there! You had me half scared to death." Her voice sounded frantic.

"Mom ... what are you talking about?"

"Get up and turn on the television!"

"Can't you tell me over the phone for cripes sake?"

"They're rioting in Detroit. Lock the doors and stay in the house!"

"Who is?'

"Those damned ... blacks! They're burning the town down."

My mother knew I was hanging out with some black guy from work, and she didn't like it one bit, but she chose to avoid a useless confrontation. Now she had visions of a Zulu uprising with me in the middle of it. She would have had a coronary had she known where I had spent my evening. "Calm down! I'll turn on the news after I go to the toilet."

"I'll be home as soon as I can get there."

I had been enjoying the prospect of having the house to myself for the rest of the week. "Stay at Aunt Silvia's until Saturday like you planned. Nothing is going on here. I'm looking out my window and all I see is Mr. Bronkowski washing his car, and all I can hear are the birds chirping. It's like a damn Disney movie over here, Mom, so relax."

"Are you sure, son?"

"Positive! I'll call you if there's a problem. Everything is fine here."

"I don't want you going down there. Promise me!"

"I promise!"

"Don't go to work either!"

"Mom, you're driving me crazy. I've got a few more days off. Don't worry. Everything will be fine."

"Are you sure?"

"I'm sure. Stay in Port Huron; I'll call you every day."

"I love you."

"Yeah, I love you, Mom. Bye!"

"Promise me!"

"I promise. Bye, Ma!"

I hung up the phone and walked downstairs to turn on the television and get some breakfast. Every local channel was running continuous news coverage as events unfolded.

A blind pig, an after-hours drinking club above Economy Printing on 12th Street, had been raided early Sunday morning. A party was being given for a black veteran who had just returned from Vietnam, and the party had stretched into the early morning hours. The size of the gathering took the Detroit police by surprise. The 10th Precinct cleanup squad called for extra patrol cars and an extra paddy wagon to arrest and transport eighty-two patrons of the blind pig to the police station for booking. Police procedure required that men and women be transported separately which made enough time for an unruly crowd to develop. Shortly before 5:00 AM, a group of Saturday-night holdovers, street people, and street toughs began to harass the police as the last of the prisoners was being loaded up. Amid angry curses, a liquor bottle flew from the crowd and shattered a squad car window. The police commissioner had ordered the police not to use their guns. When the crowd realized this, the battle began.

Word went out quickly from the neighborhood that all hell was breaking loose on 12th Street. An irrational exuberance gripped the growing crowd. At about 8:30 AM, the first alarm went out to the Detroit Fire Department. A Molotov cocktail was thrown through a shoe-store window at 12th and Blaine. By this time, the crowd had swelled with local youths, mostly males, smashing windows and looting businesses. The police attempted to seal off the street to contain the rioters.

The fire chief had assembled an all-Negro firefighting force from stations throughout the city, with the hope that the crowd wouldn't harass black firefighters combating the spreading fires. Dark billows from burning businesses filled the sky as more buildings went up in flames. Captain Taylor, the highest-ranking black person in the department, was made acting fire chief of the Fourth Firefighting Battalion. *The Detroit News* quoted him as saying, "We seem to be their favorite target." The strategy hadn't worked; white or black, the rioters didn't care. Bottles, rocks, and bricks rained down on the firefighters as they fought in vain to control the rampaging blazes. An apocalyptic terror gripped the city.

Every television station repeated the same news, so I decided to phone Brooke. Her father said she was still at church, so I called Walt instead. His mother answered the phone.

"Yes dear, he's watching the news with his father. Isn't it terrible?"

"Looks pretty bad, Mrs. Dunwoody."

"I just don't understand how people can act like that ... burning their own neighborhood. White people would never do that!" she said with an elemental certitude borne of benign ignorance.

"Let's hope not, Mrs. Dunwoody. Can I talk to Walt?"

"Just a second, dear."

Walt's mother didn't work and had probably never known a black person personally in her whole life. Despite what she said, I felt she was convinced she knew everything she had to about "those people." They were savages who should be put on a boat and sent back to Africa.

"Hey, man! The natives were restless last night. Those jungle bunnies are swinging from the trees today."

I should have known better than to call Walt. "It looks pretty serious," I said.

"What's up?"

"My mom's gone and I thought you might like to watch the television coverage over here."

"Funny thing! I was thinking about calling some people and having a riot party over here. What do you think?"

"That's repulsive!"

"Lighten up, Jake! What difference does it make what happens to those ignorant assholes?"

"Those 'ignorant assholes' are human beings. It makes me sick what's happening."

"The cops better stop them before it spreads to this neighborhood."

"I don't think we have anything to worry about."

"Oh! We're not worried. My dad loaded up his shotguns and deer hunting rifles. We're ready to go buck hunting. He's thinking about outfiting that old hearse he's been restoring and making it into a ghetto cruiser."

I couldn't believe what I was hearing.

"So, what do you say? We'll order some Kentucky Fried Chicken and some pizza and make a party out of it. I'll have my mother call Brooke's mom and invite her over too."

"I think I'll pass on it."

"What's wrong with you?"

"It turns my stomach how ignorant people can be."

"That stupid job has made a nigger lover out of you, hasn't it?"

"That's enough!" I snapped over the phone. "Walt, you've never had a tough day in your life. You snooty little shit. What gives you such a superior attitude except spending your daddy's money and lording it over the rest of us? You pathetic fuck!" I said. Then I hung up on him.

I tried calling Brooke thirty minutes later, but her

father wouldn't let her leave the house or even talk to me over the phone. Word had spread already that I ran with niggers and wasn't fit to date a decent white girl like his daughter.

A siege mentality had gripped the entire Metro Detroit area by this time. I was so agitated that I spent the rest of the day alone watching news of the unfolding tragedy. The local news people looked shell-shocked because they were not equipped to handle a story this huge and volatile. On the local ABC affiliate, WXYZ, channel ten's sports anchor, Dave Diles, reluctantly read the weekend's sports news, "though there hardly seems to be a point to it today," he said.

My mom couldn't stay away; by late afternoon, she returned home frazzled but glad our neighborhood and house were not aflame. After all, we were less than ten miles from the rioting, and the city hadn't been sealed off yet.

It had been a tough afternoon for the Detroit police. The chief decided to sweep 12th Street with a tactic that had worked a year earlier to break up a smaller insurrection. In riot gear, the police formed a phalanx. The cops hoped to break up the mob and crush the swelling rebellion. They marched with military precision through the middle of the street, but the mob simply parted and swept in behind them. The mob had done what Alexander the Great had done to the

Persians, Hannibal had done to the Romans, and Hitler had done to the French and their allies. They had outmaneuvered their enemy. The failed strategy was comical and only emboldened the rioters.

In a desperate attempt to forestall more violence, black leaders tried to calm the swelling crowds. Black congressman John Conyers, using a bull horn from the roof of a parked car, pleaded with the crowd to disassemble and go home. He was lucky to escape with his life, even with police protection, as the rioters chased him from their neighborhood.

At 1:42 PM, a call went out from a fire company on 12th Street, to fire department headquarters: "Emergency! Emergency! Get us some police protection immediately!" An anguished and terse reply came crackling back, "Nothing available." By late afternoon, a call went out from the fire department that had not been used since its inception in 1943 after a race riot during World War II, signal 3-777, the instant recall of all Detroit firefighters.

As the afternoon stretched into early evening, Governor George Romney ordered four hundred state troopers and the first units of the Michigan National Guard into action. The riot was spreading unchecked. Plate-glass windows shattered as young and old, male and female, black and white, began emptying stores in an orgy of looting and arson. To make matters worse, a second front had opened up on Detroit's East Side. Mack Avenue erupted. Detroit's inner city was ablaze and out of control. Romney took a helicopter tour to survey the damage. "It looks like a city that has been bombed," he announced, as he slapped a 9:00 PM curfew on city residents which was ignored by most people. At 3:00 AM, the governor called United States Attorney General Ramsey Clark for federal paratroopers.

After an agonizing twenty-four hours, the United States military, for the first time in history, prepared to secure the streets of a major American city, an assignment they had hoped they would never get. Most of the troops were battle hardened, fresh from a tour of duty in Vietnam. They looked out of place in full battle dress, riding city buses into the charred, smoldering streets. It was early Tuesday morning. By Tuesday night, an uneasy calm had settled over the East Side. On the West Side, a gun battle raged. By Wednesday, the official death toll stood at twenty-five.

Martial law had been declared late Sunday, but it didn't quell the "civil disturbance," as the politicians called it. The word "riot" was inflammatory in itself and city officials hesitated to use it. But that was the word on everybody's lips. There had been riots in Watts in Los Angeles and in the city of Newark, but neither compared to the carnage and wanton destruction of Detroit's riot. Snipers kept the police at bay, and firefighters were unable to get the burning city under control. Soon, the fires were left to burn themselves out. Looters had another field day.

The local and national news services did their best

to report on the riot, but they were in as much danger as everyone else from snipers and roving gangs. Rumors were rampant in the communities surrounding Detroit, which contributed to the general hysteria. One such rumor was that busloads of blacks were driving up from Toledo to help their brothers in the struggle against the white man's oppression. False reports circulated that Eastland and Westland Shopping Centers were on fire and gangs of rioters were heading into suburban neighborhoods.

The hysteria cut predictably along racial lines, fanning long-held prejudices and hatreds. Big-mouthed bigots were in their glory; Southeastern Michigan was an armed camp where paranoia ruled. "Peace-loving" families loaded their hunting guns and sharpened their knives. Handguns came out of night-stands and closets. Even baseball bats with bolts driven into their ends evoked primitive images of primal fear. Most suburbanites huddled in their remote neighborhoods and waited for the storm to pass, but others prepared for hand-to-hand combat much the same as a shadow boxer jabs at the faceless darkness before him.

After the first day of the riot, ammunition was hard to come by. Suburban gun shops had sold out their stocks. There was a run at grocery stores on bottled water, alcohol, food, batteries, and cigarettes. Frightened people hoarded anything that might be useful; store shelves emptied despite price gouging by many of the city's merchants. In an attempt to control the frenzy, Governor Romney banned alcohol and gasoline sales throughout the Detroit area.

Suburban Detroit's worst nightmare was being played out in local and national news reports on their televisions and radios. The national stories centered on the disputes between Michigan government officials and the federal government. The Johnson administration was reluctant to commit federal troops to the city streets, and he was critical of local governments for not being able to handle their own problems. It wasn't until Wednesday that the troops were in place, but order had yet to be restored.

14

The Dark Wood of Error

The midnight shift on Thursday was my next scheduled day to work. I was reasonably certain I wouldn't have any problem getting there. Zug Island was in the south end of town, away from the riot area. The 9:00 PM curfew was still in effect, and my mother nagged me to stay home, with no success.

"What's a matter with you? Do you have some kind of death wish?"

"There's nothing to worry about. President Johnson called the troops out."

"So, what does that tell you? Call in sick tonight! I don't want you going back to that snake pit."

"I'll get fired."

"Quit!"

My mother was afraid someone might murder me in the dark. She had never felt comfortable with me working there in the first place. To her, my job was as much a punishment as it was a way to earn money. The fact that I referred to Theo as my friend didn't sit well with her either. The riots magnified every trumped-up fear she ever had about black people.

But I had gone way beyond the fear of working with these guys; they were friends with names and faces. My coworkers were just regular people trying to scratch out a living like everybody else, and I was worried about their safety. Being stuck at home for four days watching nonstop news coverage with no information on my work buddies was wearing on me.

"I'm not quitting. I've got a month to go yet."

"It's after curfew. You'll get arrested!" she insisted.

"I don't think so," I said grabbing my lunch bag. "I'll see you in the morning if I don't work a double. Don't worry."

"The money isn't worth your life!" was her final remark as I walked out the side door to the driveway.

I was concerned about how the guys were doing, especially Theo. I was afraid he couldn't resist going down to the riot areas and being part of the action, and I hoped he wasn't that foolish. He didn't have a phone where I could reach him, and I had never given him my phone number. It was a telling realization of a limitation I had placed upon our relationship.

I took my usual route up Oakwood Boulevard, to Fort Street, and right onto Dearborn Street. The lighted roads were near empty, and the hushed highway echoed the sounds of my Bug's exhaust pipes. Before I crossed over to West Jefferson, I was stopped by soldiers who were barring entrance into town from the south. Three combat veterans drew down on me with their M-16's and ordered me out of the car. An armored vehicle was parked in the middle of the intersection with a mounted machine gun pointed at my windshield—a real attention grabber.

My mother was right to worry. I was in danger, but not from rioters or the guys I worked with. The authorities worried me more at the moment. These soldiers were battle-hardened troops, fresh from Nam, and they had sealed off the city. They had their orders.

"Out of the car and put your hands on your head. Now!" one of the soldiers said as he motioned with his assault rifle to make his point. I wasn't about to argue with him.

"What are you doing out here, sir?" said another combat soldier, who couldn't have been over twenty. "Out of the vehicle, sir." My nickname had gone from "son" to "kid" to "sir." *Is that a promotion?* For some reason, that idea struck me as funny. Nerves probably. "Do you find this humorous, sir?"

"No," I said, getting serious. "I'm going to work."

"You know that martial law has been declared?"

"Except for people going to work. That's what the local news reported tonight."

The other soldiers checked inside my car and saw my hardhat and work clothes. They searched my lunch bag and left the wax paper loose on my baloney sandwich. "Open your trunk, sir."

Oh, boy! Here we go again. I pulled the latch from inside, and they lifted the hood. "Lieutenant, look here." I couldn't imagine what would capture their attention from my trunk until I saw one of the soldiers take out two six-packs of empty pop bottles I hadn't taken back to the store for deposit. "What are you going to do with these?"

"Redeem them."

"Sorry, sir. I need to confiscate them."

"They're just empties."

"They can be filled with gasoline and made into Molotov cocktails, sir."

"For twenty-four cents, be my guest. You can have them."

"You're free to go, sir," the young soldier said waving me through the roadblock with the M-16 resting on his hip. I thanked him and considered myself damned lucky and drove off without delay.

All the street lamps in Delray had been broken out, so in the middle of the night, my headlights cut through the darkness like I was driving in a tunnel. Halfway to the back entrance of the island, the darkness was broken by the red revolving lights from a squad car parked diagonally on the sidewalk.

As far as I could tell in the dark, two cops in riot gear were working over a black guy who was protecting his head from their flailing nightsticks. They backed him into a recessed storefront and kneed him in the groin. He doubled over trying to protect his head and body with his forearms. Seeing him hunched up on the sidewalk, I thought, *Poor bastard. I'm glad it's not me.* I went about my business and drove until I entered the island. I was relieved to have made it safely, despite my mother's warranted warnings. I found a parking space not far from the clock house, punched in, went to the coke ovens, and waited for the shift to begin.

Now that I had witnessed firsthand some of the senseless violence, I worried how the crew might react to me because of the riot. I entered the break room and found a place to stand among guys sprawled out all over the benches and tables. Many of them hadn't been home since the riot began because they lived in the stricken areas and weren't anxious to get home. Some didn't have a home to go back to. They worked as much as possible and stayed in the break room the rest of the time, listening to the radio for the latest news until they fell asleep. Their expressions ranged from worry and despair to anger and frustration. I looked around for Theo, but he hadn't arrived yet. He lived outside the riot areas, so he had to pass by an armed checkpoint also.

Alonzo Sanchez wasn't concerned or worried over the riot. He was in an exceptional mood. During the height of the riots, he was busy looting and bartering stolen property. He always had something going on the side, and most of the crew tolerated him as long as he kept his business under control. But nobody was in a mood to tolerate any of his shit this night. To them, it was one thing to be a two-bit drug pusher and quite another to be taking advantage of their personal tragedy.

"Anyone need a color TV? How about a fancy Italian suit or some shoes? I hope this riot never ends, I'm going to make me a fortune," he boasted.

The Rev was one of the most respected men at the plant. He was elderly and smoked cheap, smelly cigars to their butt ends, but it was his only vice. He didn't openly preach; he was more of a blue-collar philosopher. He walked up to Alonzo and quietly advised him to keep his business to himself. Alonzo made a huge mistake. He turned on Rev. "Mind your own fucking business, preacher man!"

Pent-up emotions were running high, and several men grabbed Alonzo roughly and dragged him out of the break room. Sarge strode over and rescued him before Alonzo got his ass seriously kicked. They left him shaken but defiant, cursing the whole lot of them. He wiped some blood from his split lip and vowed to get his gun out of his locker and shoot the next black bastard who gave him any shit.

At that, Sarge snapped and pulled a .45 Browning semiautomatic from his waistband, the same sidearm he had used in Korea. "You want some of this, you bottom-feeding son of a bitch?" he raged grasping Alonzo's jacket and sticking the barrel of his service revolver under the Cuban's jaw. Sarge was one of the guys who didn't have a house to go back to; in fact, he didn't have a neighborhood to go back to. Several men struggled to pull him off Alonzo. It took all of them to wrestle the gun away and restrain him. "Start running, you sleazy bastard, and don't let me catch you around here again. Stop at your locker and you're a dead man!"

Alonzo, thinking he was safely away, turned around and gave Sarge the finger. "Fuck you, nigger!"

That was it. Sarge broke free like a man possessed and chased Alonzo past the locker room, down the canteen road, over the railroad tracks, and into the parking lot. Sanchez jumped into his Cadillac and sped off like he had seen Satan himself. "Don't ever cross my path or you're a dead motherfucker!" Sarge shouted and then bent over to catch his breath.

By this time, the security guard in the booth had seen the Caddy fishtail out of the parking lot and wondered what was going on. "What's the deal, Sarge?"

With labored breathing, he walked over to the booth. "Jackie … if you ever … see that Pinto Bean … on the island again … call me quick. Ya hear?"

"What happened?"

"I fired the son of a bitch." He turned around and saw his crew had followed them into the parking lot. "Don't you guys … have something … better to do?"

Everyone was agitated, but nobody said a word as they began walking back toward the ovens. Only Rev hung back and waited for Sarge. "Here's your gun," he said. "I thank God you didn't use it on my account."

"God help me, I wanted to, Rev."

Walking back with the rest of the crew, I saw Theo limping from the clock house into work late. I waited for him to catch up with me. One of his eyes was swollen shut. "What happened to you?"

"My Imperial got torched Sunday night, and I had to walk to work tonight."

"Somehow I knew you'd get caught up in the rioting. So, what happened?"

"Someone threw a fire bomb through the window of my parked car."

I thought about my confiscated pop bottles. "No shit? You're lucky you weren't killed. How did you get home?"

"I hustled out of there as fast as I could."

"Why are you limping?"

"I tried taking a taxi to work, but no cabbie would bring me into town. I started walking and bumped into our friends again."

"Our friends?"

"Our crime-fightin' buddies. Frick and fuckin' Frack."

Suddenly it struck me who the cops were working

over, and I went numb. I hoped he hadn't seen me drive past him. It was dark and tough to recognize anyone because the cops were all over the poor guy. *What could I have done anyway?* I rationalized. *At least I can be a witness if it goes to court.*

"File a police brutality report," I suggested, trying to ease my guilt.

"Sure! A black man with no witnesses during a race riot. I don't think so."

"I saw them," I confessed. "I didn't know who they were beating until now, but I saw them."

"Me or someone else, what does it matter? It's open season on niggers. Especially now."

"Sad but true." I realized how hollow and helpless the truth can sound. I felt guilty, and my face must have shown it.

Theo let me off the hook. "There's nothing you could have done, my friend. Besides, I've got other things on my mind," he said pausing. "I called Memphis earlier tonight. My wife talked to me this time."

"Really? Well, that's something, I guess."

"She's been watching the riot news on the national news and was worried about me." The beating he just took paled in the light of knowing his estranged wife was worried about him. "I'm going back to try to work something out with her," he said. "I want to get my life back together. I want to be a family again. Try to be a father to my son."

"So you've decided to return home?"

"Why not! You'll be quitting in a few weeks. It won't be much fun around here after you leave. I'll just have to break in some other asshole."

"Watch it now! You're sounding like Lester the Molester." We shared a mild chuckle and walked quietly the rest of the way to the coke oven battery.

I hadn't talked about quitting because I had mixed feelings about it. It was inevitable that I'd go back to college because my mom had willed it so, but I felt some appreciation and affection for the working-class life, with all of its crude vulgarity and harsh reality. I had a better understanding of the challenges my father faced as a young man with no education and an infant son. College seemed artificial to me now, not the real world. I wasn't sure I would feel comfortable there, but I needed to return, if not for me, then for my mother and the memory of my father.

My mother's disappointment with me wasn't only about family pride; it ran much deeper. She and my father never finished high school and always struggled to make ends meet. They wanted me to have a career and feared I would fall under the allure of easy money and head down the wrong path. The summer of 1967 was an eye-opener.

"When do you think you'll be leaving for Memphis?" I asked.

"I'm pretty much played out here," he said, wiggling a loose tooth and spitting some blood. "When are you quitting?"

"I haven't set an exact date, so it really doesn't matter that much to me. How about the end of the next pay period? That'll give us time to put in our notice."

"Sounds like a plan!"

We worked most of August, but the job seemed more monotonous and toilsome after the riots. The entire crew went through the motions of their jobs without the usual jokes and ribbing that made the unpleasant jobs and difficult working conditions tolerable. The camaraderie was replaced with pessimism about the future. Like many of Detroit's ravaged neighborhoods, some of these men wouldn't fully recover. Alonzo never returned to work and became part of the unwritten history of the island.

The people who suffered the most were the people in the ravaged areas. Some businesses had written "Soul Brother" on their boarded-up storefronts, but that didn't necessarily save their buildings. Entire blocks went up in flames, leaving local residents without jobs or places to live. The area became even more impoverished than it was before. Immediately, business investment in the charred communities evaporated, perpetuating chronic patterns of poverty. The slogan "Black Power," painted in violet on 12th Street, stood in contrast to the devastation all around.

Once the curfew was lifted, but before order had been fully restored, city officials were outraged when carloads of sightseers from Metro Detroit, many with their kids in the backseats, cruised the ravaged neighborhoods putting themselves and others unwittingly in danger. A macabre carnival atmosphere developed as suburbanites wanted to see the carnage for themselves.

The statistics for the two-week period, the official duration of the riot, remains a legacy that Detroiters will never forget in the collective memory of the city: 43 reported deaths; 7,000 arrests; over 4,000 injuries; 2,500 buildings looted or burned to the ground; 5,000 residents left homeless; 16,682 fire runs; and a river of fire ten blocks long. The dream of a "Model City," a term said to be coined in this town by Henry Ford II, became an ironic nightmare.

In 1805, a fire had destroyed every building in the city but one. The man who organized the relief effort was a priest named Father Gabriel Richard. He had been heard to mutter these words in Latin, which would become the official motto for the city of Detroit, "*Speramus meliora resurget cineribus.*" Now, more than ever, it had a poignant significance: "We hope for better things. It shall rise from the ashes."

Over and Out

"*So when did you* think you were going to tell me?"

"Tell you what?" I asked tossing some socks into my open sports bag lying on my bed.

"I knew it would happen sooner or later. I just wish you'd be honest with me for once rather than finding out secondhand. That's all. Is that asking too much?"

"Mom! I'm going to Ypsi for a few days to catch up with some friends of mine. Classes start in two weeks. I thought I'd hand deliver my tuition payment to the cashier and reacquaint myself with the campus."

"That's all?" she probed.

"Mom, you worry too much," I said trying to smother the conversation. I wasn't sure what was on her mind, but I knew it wouldn't be long before I found out.

"Worry too much! Mark told me what you've been up to all summer. You're lucky you're not dead!"

"Not as lucky as Mark's going to feel when I get ahold of him. He's around here more than I am."

"Exactly!"

This conversation rankled me, so I anchored it with the truth. "Okay, I didn't want to worry you, but here it is. I'm going to Memphis for a quick road trip, and I'll be back in a few days."

"Memphis?" she scrunched up her face. "What in heaven's sake for?"

"Friendship. I'm driving a work buddy home who quit the same day I did." I waited for my mother to respond.

"This Theo character, no doubt?"

"Yes, why not?" I should have known better than to bait my mother.

"Now I'm positive you have a death wish," she said morosely. After losing my brother and my father, I was the last of her immediate family, except for my aunt.

"What do you mean, death wish? You're overreacting again." That set off the Irish in her.

"After what just happened in this town? Do I have to spell it out for you?"

"Maybe you do!"

Exasperated she began, "Do you remember Viola Luizzo?"

"Who?"

"Didn't you learn anything from high school?"

"Not if it happened after 1945."

"Viola Luizzo was a white mother of five from Detroit who drove down to Alabama in support of the Civil Rights movement and got gunned down by the Klan. A car pulled up next to her Oldsmobile on the highway and shot her in the head twice. That was just two years ago, mister."

"Yes. I remember it now."

"She was only thirty-nine and left five children to grow up without a mother. She had no business going down there, and neither do you!"

"That's your opinion. White people killed her."

"When you're dead, it doesn't matter who killed you."

"Mom, we're going to Memphis, not Selma or Montgomery. I'm just helping a friend. That's all!"

"That's what Viola was doing," she countered.

"Gotta go, Mom."

"Before you leave, there is something I want to tell you."

Now what? I was weary of this conversation, and I needed to get going. I zipped up my bag and motioned to leave.

"I've decided to list the house and move in with your aunt."

"What?" I heard her words, but they weren't registering.

"You've already left the nest; now go fly."

"What?"

"I know you've been looking for a place in Ypsilanti."

"So this is what this is all about? Okay, Mom, you can drop the guilt trip."

"No, son, you've become a martyr to your own self-will."

"All right! I admit I've made a few mistakes."

"A few?" she said raising her eyebrows. "But you know how to take care of yourself, so it's time I started taking care of myself. I need a change of scenery."

"You're serious."

"It's been on my mind for awhile. See me when you return, and give me your new address and a phone number where I can contact you."

Caught off balance, I said, "I'll see what I can do."

"Don't disappoint me!" she said clutching me softly and kissing me on the cheek.

Stunned, I heard the screen door slam and I quietly swore, "Son of a bitch."

Through the open kitchen window, I heard my mother's voice say, "And another thing—watch that mouth of yours!"

Those last few weeks Theo and I worked together,

we didn't talk much about where our individual paths would lead. There was always a no man's land that separated us, whether we admitted it or not, but there was also a stronger common bond that drew us into the same orbit that eventful summer. Maybe it was the curious attraction of opposites. I hope not; I just liked the guy. It was my good fortune that we had met, but somehow it didn't seem enough.

We quit at the end of the August pay period after our two-week notice was up, assured that our last checks would be mailed to us. I had two weeks before college began in mid-September, and I was starting to look forward to the crisp autumn days on campus. I had a prefabricated future of tests to take and papers to write; of minimum wage, part-time jobs to tolerate; and a profession to jump hoops through. Everything considered, I looked forward to being a university student again.

Theo felt edgier about his future for understandable reasons. He had come north to make money and improve the lives of his family. Now nothing was going right. All he knew was that he wanted his family back. Theo didn't want his son, Otis, to grow up without a father as he had. A boy needs a father: someone to play catch with and catch hell from. He remembered his parentless childhood and wanted to do right by his son. The atmosphere after the riots made returning home an easier decision for him to make.

That bombshell my mom had just dropped on me was a real blockbuster. But after my initial surprise, I felt relieved and grinned. I looked forward to my independence.

I turned the key and my Bug rumbled alive. I threw it in gear and drove to Theo's boarding house and found him sitting on the porch steps waiting for me. This time I was the one who was late. Theo's lanky body was half folded as he hunched his arms on his knees and watched the traffic go by. He had on a pair of brown polished dress shoes; some tan, lightweight gabardine dress slacks; and an open-collared, yellow tropical shirt. He looked too good to be traveling seven hundred miles on a bus. His battered, steel-sided suitcase was crammed with all the worldly possessions he chose to keep. Clothes, mostly, I imagined. He donated what he couldn't pack of his shoes and clothing to his church for their relief effort after the riots.

My V-Dub swooped in front of his boarding house. I leaned on my horn to annoy him one last time. I should have known better—he was happy and grinned while lugging his huge suitcase down the walk to the car. "What do you have in there? Gold bars?" I greeted him.

"Not much ... just my whole life."

I knew that the suitcase wouldn't fit in my front trunk; I had my things in there. "Squeeze that bad boy into the backseat," I said.

He wrestled it through the small door opening and the tilted passenger seat. "Damned foreign cars," he muttered as the suitcase fell onto the rear bench seat. Then, he scrunched his six-foot frame into the front seat. "Hey, let's hit it! The bus leaves in fifteen minutes," he said looking straight ahead. "Take me to the Greyhound station."

I reached across to the glove box and took out a small package. "Before we take off, I have something for you."

"What's this?"

"Something to remember me by. A token of our friendship," I said handing it to him.

He was taken aback for a moment.

"Open it up!"

Theo slowly opened the box. "A watch," he said examining and putting it on his wrist. "Same as my last one."

"Maybe you'll hang on to this one."

"Hey, man ... sorry I didn't get you anything."

"Working on the Island was a life-changing experience for me. You opened my eyes to another side of life, and I have to thank you for that."

"Glad I could oblige," he said with a fake smirk, not wanting to show any real emotion.

"Seriously, I learned a lot from you in the last eight months."

"About what? Slumming?"

"No, fool!" Theo was toying with me, but I wanted

to say my piece before we went our separate ways. "Life isn't black-and-white, right or wrong. People aren't simply black or white either; they're just good or bad. That's all! I plan to make it my business to recognize the difference." In all likelihood, we would never see each other again, so I felt I had to say something. "You changed my life, bro'," I said bumping fists with him, which seemed oddly formal though I thought the occasion called for it.

"We did have some good times."

"We certainly did."

"Yes, we did." We both grinned to fight back our emotions. I wanted to tell him I would never forget him or the crazy times we spent together, but that would have been too much. "Are you ready to roll?"

"Son, I was born ready."

"I figured that," I said as I revved the engine and made my Bug leap away from the curb. I drove in the direction of the downtown Greyhound station but suddenly turned left onto Dearborn Street.

"Where you going, Jake? This is the wrong direction."

I drove to the freeway entrance and turned south down Interstate 75.

"Turn around! I'll be late for my bus."

"No you won't! I'm tired of driving up West Jefferson. In fact, it'll be a long time before I drive up West Jefferson again, so I'm driving you back home in style on a salt-and-pepper cruise. I've got some time to kill, and I'm not thrilled about hanging around the neighborhood until my classes start. Any objections?"

"You must be out of your cotton-pickin' mind!" He grinned.

"It's a fine madness," I said as we motored past Melvindale and its gasoline storage tanks.

Forty years later, I found a hand-addressed business envelope in my mailbox along with the usual bills, junk mail, and catalogues. The envelope had a Memphis return address, and I hesitated before opening it until I was finished going through everything else. I found myself reading through the *Pennysaver,* which usually goes directly into the trash. Then I looked at the envelope for a moment before I slit it open with my pocketknife. Inside was a beautifully handwritten letter from Thelma Thomas, a person I didn't know then but do now, and another sealed, letter-sized envelope with my name written on it with pencil in a hand I recognized.

Dear Mister Malone,

I am writing you this letter on behalf of my grandfather, Theodore Semple, who died last month from complications of emphysema. He often talked about you and the good times you two had working together in Detroit. I think he exaggerated them somewhat, but his stories never failed to make us laugh. His family misses him greatly.

I thought you might like to know that my grandfather's son, Otis, had three children. I am Thelma, the oldest, and I became an elementary school teacher. Aaron became an accountant, and Joseph became a divinity student and is the pastor of his own congregation in town. My grandfather was very proud of us all.

When Grandfather returned from Detroit, he got a job busing tables and washing dishes in a Creole restaurant, where he learned the business in no time. The owner was old and became ill, so he sold the business after a few years to my grandfather who set up his own BBQ place called Smokin' Joe's Rib Shack. When he started to slow down, his son—my father—took over the business and turned it into a small chain of shops throughout the Memphis area. Maybe you've heard our advertising slogan, "Our Ribs are Finger-Suckin' Good." My grandfather thought that one up himself.

Acting on my grandfather's written wishes, he wanted you to have his wristwatch, which seems to have disappeared. We believe one of our cousins stole and pawned it. There is one in every family. Grandfather also had this envelope among his personal things which has your name on it.

After some searching on the Internet, I was able to find your address and send it along. There were a number of Jacob Malones in the Michigan online directory but only one Jake. I am confident that you are the right person. If not, please return it to me.

My grandfather told me of your fondness for Southern home cooking. If you are ever in the Memphis area, please drop by and have some sweet potato pie and ribs with us. We'll treat you right. I'd like to hear some stories about my grandfather. He often said you were his best friend.

Sincerely,
Thelma (Semple) Thomas

My instincts about the letter were correct. I knew what it was about before I had opened it, so I was prepared. I looked at the smaller envelope and carefully slit it open. Inside was a worn, faded photograph of Theo's father in his army uniform standing in front of a potted palm tree. I could see the son in the father and the father in the son, and out of the blue I made the sign of the cross.

CPSIA information can be obtained
at www.ICGtesting.com
Printed in the USA
FFOW03n2053280114
3319FF